Rick Patterson had never expected to see the inside of a jail. He'd learned living the hard way and while he wasn't afraid of knocks, he knew you didn't have to go seeking them out either. That that came to you, you dealt with. But a man was a fool not to avoid trouble if he could. And people were trouble.

Without knowing it, Rick was a lonely man. Maybe that's why he tied in with an old coot like Deuce Taylor. Deuce had lived past his time—and knew it. Rick didn't mind the old mountain man's blowhard stories—he figured Taylor had a lot of bottom to him underneath all that talk, and he figured to learn all Taylor could teach him.

It turned out to be a lot more than he'd figured —because Taylor wasn't one to run from a vicious battle with the Cattle Association, and eventually, Rick got to feel the same way.

And by the time he caught up with himself, it was a lot of years, and a lot of dead men later.

And he was in jail for murder.

YOU'LL NEVER HANG ME

Lee Leighton

BALLANTINE BOOKS • **NEW YORK**

All rights reserved. Published in the United States by Ballantine
Books, a division of Random House, Inc., New York, and
simultaneously in Canada by Random House of Canada,
Limited, Toronto, Canada.

ISBN 0-345-29119-0

Manufactured in the United States of America

First Edition: September 1971
Second Printing: May 1981

YOU'LL NEVER HANG ME

1

Pat Brady had just finished eating breakfast in his living quarters back of his print shop when he heard someone pounding on the street door. The sun was barely showing over the continental divide, too early for anyone to be bringing news to the Elk City Weekly Gazette. Besides, Rick Patterson's hanging wasn't scheduled until noon and that was the only big news around Elk City right now.

Swearing, Brady strode the length of the print shop to the front door, unlocked it, and jerked it open. Deputy John Ash stood there, unshaven and red-eyed from lack of sleep, his face holding the same mean expression it usually did, or meaner if possible.

"Must take some mighty important news to bring you banging around here before the sun's up," Brady grumbled. "Or is it up?"

"Dunno," Ash said. "I ain't got my eyes open wide enough to tell. I've been sitting up guarding Patterson all night. Soon as we string him up, I'm going to bed and sleep for a week. He wants to see you."

"Who?"

"Patterson."

"What the hell for?"

"Dunno," Ash answered. "Just get your tail over to the jail. The sheriff says to give the condemned man all the favors we can. If it was me, I wouldn't give him the time of day, but that's what Ole says."

Ash swung around and strode back across the street to the courthouse. Brady watched him for a few seconds, wondering what Patterson wanted, then he shrugged, took his derby off the antler rack, and clapped it on his head.

It would be another hot day, he thought as he started across the street, hot and dry and crackling with the kind of tension that scared a man. There wouldn't be any trouble over the hanging, he told himself. He'd been telling himself that for days. Still, you never knew.

Brady paused for a moment when he reached the boardwalk in front of the courthouse, his gaze on the scaffold that had been completed only the night before. He had always been amused by the irony of stories he'd heard about convicted prisoners looking out of their cell windows and watching the scaffold being erected on which they would hang. It wasn't true in this case. The sheriff's office and county jail were on the west side of the courthouse, and the scaffold was on the east side.

A hanging just naturally attracted a crowd. It would today, too. Within two or three hours Main Street would be lined on both sides with saddle horses and teams and rigs. The boardwalks would be crowded with farmers and ranchers.

A good many of the visitors, wanting to be here on time, were already camped along the creek above town. The stores and saloons would do a land office business. Brady had heard the night before that the hotel had every room filled for the first time in more than ten years.

Brady considered the morbid curiosity that was a part of nearly every human being, then shrugged his shoulders and paused in front of the courthouse, admitting to himself that the crowd today would be attracted by more than morbid curiosity. Public feeling after Rick Patterson's conviction for murdering fourteen-year-old Davey Lamond had run so high that for a time it seemed he wouldn't live long enough to hang legally.

The threatened raid on the jail had not taken place because Sheriff Ole Swanson was a square-jawed Swede who never backed away from anything. He announced that the first man who tried breaking Patterson out of jail either to lynch him or free him would get hell shot out of him. He hired more deputies who took turns standing guard at the jail. The tough talk stopped, largely because Swanson had the reputation of doing exactly what he said he would.

When Brady glanced at the scaffold, he saw that Ash and Swanson were standing beside it. On impulse he walked toward them, calling, "Think it'll work?"

Swanson swung around, peered at him in the thin dawn light for a moment, then he grunted, "Oh, it's you. Yeah, it'll work. I suppose you're here bright and early to get a front seat."

"No, Ole," Brady said. "I'll report the hanging in the next issue of the Weekly Gazette, but I refuse to print the lurid details. I figure about two lines will do it. Won't be necessary to tell any more than that, seeing as everybody in the county will be here to enjoy the spectacle."

Ash swore and said, "That's a fact."

Swanson glared at Brady, then chewed on his cigar butt and spat at the nearest clump of dog fennel. "Thought I told John to tell you to get over to the jail. Patterson wants to see you."

"What about?"

"Didn't say. He's a cool son of a bitch. Wouldn't see the preacher. Said he wasn't worried about going to hell. Just wants to see you and Ed Vernal." Swanson scratched his chin, then said, "You boys figuring to bust him out of jail, put him on a horse, and let him ride to freedom while you and Vernal shoot it out with me and my deputies?"

Brady didn't like Swanson and he was quite aware that Swanson didn't like him, but now he couldn't keep from grinning. "That's pretty poor humor, Sheriff," he said. "I have no intention of barring the smooth path of justice, even though I think this is a hell of a miscarriage of the justice you lawmen and lawyers like to talk about."

"Most ways, Brady, you're a tolerably intelligent man for an editor," Swanson said, "but you're a complete idiot on this. There was never the least doubt about Patterson's guilt from the day John brought him in, but you started weaseling around about the bastard even before the trial."

"He's not the kind who would kill a boy," Brady said. "I've talked to him more than anyone else except Vernal,

and I've got to know him pretty well. It took the Cattlemen's Association a long time to get him, but looks like
they'll finally make it, and it'll look legal."

"It is legal, damn it," Swanson said angrily, "and the
Cattlemen's Association had nothing to do with it. Patterson had a fair trial. I say you're a fool. John, take him
over to the jail. Let's not keep Patterson waiting on his
last morning on earth."

"Did the Association pass the word down to you to be
sure that Patterson didn't get out of this alive?" Brady
asked.

The question jolted Swanson, not much, but enough to
make Brady think that was exactly what had happened. If
not the Association, then some of the individual members
who had enough wealth and power to be listened to had
made contact with the sheriff, possibly some who lived
right here in the county. Not that it could be proved.
Patterson had said it from the first, and it had made sense
to Brady then and still did.

For just a moment Swanson didn't know quite how to
take it or what to do, then his face turned red and he
clenched his right fist and lifted it to hit Brady. A few
seconds later he dropped it back to his side, saying, "Get
him over to the jail before I kill him," and, turning his
back to Brady, stalked away.

"Come along," Ash said, his face almost as red with
anger as Swanson's, "or maybe I'll kill you myself. That
was a hell of a thing to say to Ole."

"Wasn't it now," Brady agreed.

There was no way to save Patterson with his hanging
only hours away, but Brady felt a wave of regret for not
starting along this path in the beginning. He might have
forced the sheriff and maybe even the judge into making a
mistake, or at least getting a life sentence for Patterson.

The defending lawyer had done a poor job, acting as if
he were whipped before the trial started. Everyone in the
county except Brady and Vernal thought Patterson was
guilty, and the lawyer who had come from Cheyenne was
probably just as convinced of his guilt as anyone.

Ash didn't say a word as they made the half-circle of

the courthouse to the west door that led into the sheriff's office and county jail. Opening the heavy iron door into the block of cells, he called, "Sam, the boss says to let the inkslinger see Patterson and not keep him waiting on his last day on earth."

Sam Briscoe had made it tough on Patterson ever since he'd been arrested. He was a small man who was always scared enough of his prisoners to be dangerous. He sat in the corridor, a double-barreled shotgun across his lap. He scowled at Brady, then yelled at Ash, "John, you search him for a gun?"

"No," Ash answered. "I was hoping he'd have one. Then if he tried to give it to Patterson, you'd have reason to shoot both of 'em."

"I'd do it, too," Briscoe said, "only he might have more'n one. Between 'em they'd get me, and Patterson would walk out of here. You keep Brady covered and I'll see if he's got an iron on him."

"Oh hell," Ash said in disgust. "He ain't fool enough to try anything. It's a waste of time."

"He ain't going in there till I know," Briscoe said. "You can make up your mind to that."

Ash swore and drew his gun. He stood in the doorway holding it on Brady until Briscoe made his search, then Briscoe unlocked the door of Patterson's cell. Ed Vernal who was inside rose as soon as Brady came in.

"All yours, Mr. Editor," Vernal said. He turned to Patterson, took one long last look at the prisoner, then held out his hand. "So long, son," he said. "Good riding."

Patterson tried to grin, but his lips wouldn't accept the mental order. He said, "Watch out, Ed. Don't let any of them whorehouse girls roll you."

Vernal whirled and walked away, his face showing no emotion. He was a stocky, bowlegged cowboy who apparently had ridden with Patterson for a long time and was his best friend. He had come from somewhere around Sundance to Elk City soon after Patterson's arrest, had taken a room on the second floor of the hotel facing the courthouse, and had testified at the trial as a character witness, saying he'd known Patterson for years and swearing that he wasn't a man who would kill a boy. No one paid the slightest attention to his testimony, and that, of course, had not surprised Brady.

As soon as Vernal left, Brady turned to Patterson. A tray of food on the floor had not been touched. Brady asked, "They send you some slop for your last breakfast?"

Patterson shrugged his shoulders. "It was all right, I guess, but it was a waste of grub. I ain't hungry. Why would anyone eat when he's gonna kick the bucket in a little while?"

"It's just a custom to give a man a good meal before they kill him," Brady said. "I got Ash's message that you wanted to see me."

Patterson nodded and, lifting one end of the thin mattress on his bunk, drew out a thick stack of paper. He said, "You're the only man except Ed I can trust with this." He laid the papers back on the mattress. "I guess it seems funny to you that a man like me who never amounted to a damn anyway you look at it wants to have his life story published."

"No, it doesn't seem funny," Brady said. "We've talked enough about it for me to understand how you feel."

They had talked about it, but only in generalities and not about what could actually be done with it. Brady had never told Patterson, but he doubted that it could be published. Still, it certainly had historical value and maybe the state historical society would want it.

However, if it was the damning testimony against the powerful Cattlemen's Association that Brady suspected it was, he had little hope that even the historical society would touch it.

"Funny thing." Patterson picked the papers up again and held them in front of him, staring at the top sheet blankly as if his thoughts were racing back over the events he had told about. "I've heard of men keeping a journal. It always seemed to me to be a bunch of hogwash, but after I ran into the invaders' camp and we got away and then they sent men after me to kill me I decided it wasn't hogwash after all."

Patterson raised his eyes to look at Brady. "You know,

I saw a side of the bastards that most folks never see. I guess most people think that because they're big and powerful they have to be good, real righteous the way they claim to be. It ain't so."

"I'll do what I can with it," Brady said.

"It ain't written as bad as you probably think," Patterson said. "I've worked on it at different times when we were holed up somewhere, but I've done most of it right here in this cell. Ed Vernal takes it a page at a time and fixes up the spelling and commas and such. He's had more book learning than I ever had a chance to get. I've been reading it after Ed brings it back. Everything that's in it is true, though Ed's changed a lot of the wording." He grinned. "Fact is, Brady, most of the wording is Ed's."

Still Patterson stood there, motionless, gray eyes on the stack of paper, a tall man with deep lines in his face that made him look years older than he claimed to be. Most of his hair was gone, and much of what remained had turned white. He reminded Brady of a great, bald headed eagle that could not survive in captivity. Finally he handed the papers to Brady, reluctantly as if he hated to part with them.

"I don't figger any man is gonna do better than his best," Patterson said. "I thank you for coming to see me, Mr. Brady. If it hadn't been for you and Ed, I'd have gone clean whacky with that Goddamned bastard of a Briscoe making life hell for me the way he has."

He held out his hand and Brady gripped it. Patterson said, "I've killed some men in my time. I guess that was what made it so tough on me in my trial. They raked up all the old killings and made it look like I was a bad man. If I had these last ten years to live over, I'd still kill every man I have. What gravels me the most is having to swing for a killing I didn't do."

The metal door of the cell swung open. "You've been here long enough, Brady," Sam Briscoe said. Seeing the papers in Brady's hands, he demanded, "What's that?"

"Some things Patterson wanted me to look at," Brady said, and walked rapidly past the deputy who was staring at him as if he suspected the editor of doing something illegal.

"Them the letters Patterson has been writing?" Briscoe demanded.

"That's it," Brady said, and walked faster across the sheriff's office.

Briscoe said something about Patterson having a lot of friends, and Brady heard Patterson snap back that it wasn't so many friends, but he had a few, and since he wasn't going to see them anymore, he'd written a lot to each of them. What was more, he didn't trust anybody except Vernal or Brady to mail them, and he'd forgotten to give them to Vernal.

Brady was outside in the sunshine then and he breathed a sigh of relief. He had not known what sort of story Patterson had told the lawmen about the writing he had been doing, but he had a strong hunch that if they knew the truth, they'd take the papers away from him and destroy them. If, as he suspected, the Association actually had been in touch with Swanson, the sheriff would know that the cattlemen would not want Patterson's story published.

He crossed the street to his office, locked the door, and sat down at his desk. He had no intention of leaving his office at noon to watch the hanging. He liked Patterson too well. He could not explain how he felt, or why.

It was just that he believed the man's story about finding the boy badly hurt, maybe dying, kneeling beside him hoping to stop the flow of blood from a thigh wound, then the boy dying. But John Ash had arrested him. Others might have believed his story if the prosecution had not raked up all the old incidents in Patterson's past in which he had been involved in killings. After the prosecution had once given him a reputation as a bad man, he didn't have a chance.

Brady straightened the sheets of paper, most of them torn from the kind of tablet a schoolboy would buy. The writing was in pencil, but it was legible and easy to read. The first page had only one paragraph and apparently had been written that morning. Patterson had probably laid it on top so Brady would read it first.

"I, Richard Patterson, have been tried and sentenced to die for a murder I did not commit. Do not talk to me of the bullshit I've heard from preachers and philosophers and poets about this being a good world of love and beauty and justice. I know different. I know from my personal experience that it is a bad world filled with greed and hatred and brutality. I've been chased and shot at because those with money to hire killers have wanted me dead so I could not testify at their trial if one was ever held, or at least could not make known to the general public what I saw when Matt Coleman and Bert Springer were murdered. Only one thing brings me some comfort at this time. They'll never hang me."

Brady shook his head as he laid the sheet of paper on the desk and picked up the second one. He began to read.

2

The Journal of Richard Patterson

I WAS FOURTEEN the summer I ran away from home. I would have left sooner if it hadn't been for my mother. I was her only child and she needed me, so I stayed until her death. How she managed to live as long as she did was a mystery to me.

My father died when I was a baby, so I don't remember him at all. I was born on a hardscrabble farm a few miles from Albany, Oregon. That was in the Willamette Valley which had lots of good land, but I guess my father had been both poor and a poor judge of soil. My mother remarried because she couldn't run the farm by herself, and she was just as bad a judge of men as my father had been of land.

My stepfather was born mean. When he got on a drinking spree which he did several times a year, he was meaner than ever. He wasn't much of a farmer, so the place made a mighty poor living for us. I did most of the work as soon as I was big enough to do anything. I guess that had a lot to do with me being the kind of man I am because I learned when I was young that nobody was going to give me anything, that I had to look out for myself because nobody else was going to, and that I'd never get anywhere by kowtowing to other people.

My stepfather could beat me, but he could never make me give in to him. When I was little, I guess he would have beaten me to death if Ma hadn't interfered. I learned not to cross him and to stay out of his way as much as I could, but there were times when I couldn't do it, so I'd get a beating. I've still got scars from those beatings.

The day I was fourteen I told myself he was never going to beat me again. I was almost as big as he was and just about as strong. I didn't want to make it hard on Ma, but I'd had all I was going to take from the bastard. I think that I had a real desire to kill him, but I never admitted it to myself.

It didn't come to a showdown until after my mother had a heart attack and died at the age of thirty-two. Poor food, hard work, and having to live with my stepfather was enough to give my mother a heart attack. The strange part of it was that I was glad when she died because she'd had a tough life and there didn't seem to be any chance of it getting better.

I didn't know much about heaven, though I'd heard the preacher speak a good word for it. In any case, I figured it had to be better than what she'd had in this life.

After the funeral was over and all the neighbors had left, my stepfather sat at the kitchen table with a whisky bottle in front of him and told me to build a fire and cook supper. Ma had been poorly for more than a year and I'd done most of the cooking lately.

I went out to the woodshed and picked up the bucksaw. I figured this was the time. From all the signs, my stepfather would be drunk in an hour or less and he'd try to beat me. I fiddled around with the saw and I guess most of an hour went by before I cut enough wood for supper.

When I carried it in and dropped it back of the stove into the woodbox, my stepfather was weaving a little in his chair. He was mean-eyed with slobber running down his chin. He said, "You were mighty damned slow with that wood. I'm going to teach you right now who's running this shebang. It's something you never did learn."

His words were slurred so it was hard to understand him, but I was used to hearing him talk that way, so I knew what he said, all right. He got up and grabbed his razor strap off the wall and started toward me, saying,

"Take your shirt off, boy. I aim for you to feel this real good."

I backed up toward the door. My stepfather had found a fine piece of straight oak and had been working on it in the evenings, shaving it down into an ax handle. It was leaning against the wall beside the door. I got my hands on it and stood with my back to the wall while he kept coming at me.

"If you don't get that shirt off, I'll give it to you right across the face," my stepfather said.

He raised his hand with the strap, but before he could swing it, I jumped at him, bringing that piece of oak straight down across the top of his skull. I guess he had a hard head. The blow should have split his skull wide open, but it didn't. He went down and out, a trickle of blood flowing across his forehead.

I stared at him for quite a while. He didn't move, and I don't know to this day whether he was the first man I killed or not, but I think he was. Anyhow, I got scared, thinking they'd get me for murder if he was dead, so I gathered up all my clothes and tied them into a bundle, took every cent of money I could find which was only about twenty dollars, and filled a sack with grub. As soon as it was dark I lit out, heading north.

Nobody ever came after me. If he lived, I guess he didn't want me around, with me being another mouth to feed. If he died, they didn't think about me doing it which isn't likely, or all the neighbors figured it was a good thing to kill him, with him being the kind of man he was. Maybe they just buried him and said he'd had a heart attack.

I didn't know the law wasn't after me, so I hid during the daytime and walked by night till I got to Portland. I wangled a job on a riverboat and wound up in The Dalles. I worked in a stable for a while, then went on to Baker. I wintered there and began feeling a little easier. A lot of cattle were being shipped to Wyoming and Montana in those days and I caught on with a trail herd headed for Montana.

I was big and strong for my age, so folks took me for

two or three years older than I was. That was one reason I always found work, along with the fact that I wasn't too proud to take any job I could get from shoveling horse manure in a livery stable to wrangling horses with a cow outfit which meant rolling out of my blankets a long time before the sun came up.

You hear a lot of stories of boys running away from home and almost starving to death and being mistreated by the men they worked for and so on. Nothing of the kind ever happened to me. Not that I had any bed of roses, but I made a living and at the time I wasn't expecting anything else.

My schooling stopped, of course, but I'd had a pretty good start before I left home. I read everything I could find from newspapers to the Bible to almanacs. Sometimes I found novels or history books in the places where I worked and I read them.

For a couple of years I wandered over most of western Montana. The year I was seventeen I got as far east as Miles City. In its earlier days Miles City or Milestown as some called it was a rough place with the soldiers and muleskinners and hide hunters, then the cowboys came and after that the railroad which is always a civilizing factor, partly because it brings in women. By the time I got there Miles City was a tolerably decent town.

I hooked on with an outfit that was floating logs down Tongue river when it was high. The work was hard and dangerous, and if I'd had good sense, I wouldn't have taken the job, but I was young enough to figure I could handle anything that came along. The funny part of it was I did.

After the job petered out, I didn't have any work for a while, but I had money in my pocket, so I didn't worry. I took a room in the McQueen House and lived pretty high on the hog. I knew I wouldn't last long living that way, but I wasn't one to think about tomorrow at that stage in my life.

As it turned out, living in the McQueen House was one of the most important things I ever did because I got acquainted with an old bird named Deuce Taylor. It was a mixed blessing, but I guess most things are. Deuce knew about everything there was to know when it came to living off the land, and he wound up teaching me a lot of things I didn't know and wouldn't have learned from most men. On the other hand, if I had never met Deuce, I wouldn't have got into the mess I did.

The way we got acquainted wasn't unusual, I guess, with as much trouble as there was in Miles City and the number of toughs that hung out in town, but it was kind of unlikely, too, because most men tried to stay out of trouble. I seemed to gravitate to any fight that came along, which was a damn fool way of operating, but I lived in a world of men and I guess above everything else I was trying to prove I was a man.

I'd just walked into the hotel bar late one afternoon when I saw this ruckus shaping up. Three hardcases had an old man backed up to the bar and they were hoorawing the hell out of him. He was wearing a broad-rimmed plainsman's hat, a dirty buckskin suit with fringe on it, and worn moccasins. He carried a knife in a beaded leather scabbard on his left side and a .45 in a tied-down holster on his right.

I'd never seen the hardcases before, which didn't mean anything because toughs of their caliber were floating in and out of Miles City all the time. I found out a few minutes later that they were horse thieves who had stolen some stock from the Cheyenne reservation south of Miles City. They'd brought the horses up here to sell, and if they'd behaved themselves, they'd have made it fine, but they got sidetracked picking on Deuce Taylor.

He had a white beard and mustache and long hair. If he'd showed up in Jim Bridger's day, nobody would have looked at him twice, but he was clean out of date. Most of the time a man dressed like Deuce was a fraud claiming by his clothes and manners to be something he wasn't. The hardcases made a mistake thinking Deuce was a phony. Still, tough old bird that he was, he couldn't have handled the three of them.

By the time I showed up, he'd had all he was going to

take from the hardcases. He said, "Boys, you've had your fun. Now let me alone."

The biggest one of the three was the ringleader, I guess. He was a giant of a man, making Deuce look like a runt which he wasn't. He leaned forward and stuck out his big jaw and said, "We ain't through funnin', old man. I wanted to know if you're Buffalo Bill. You said no, but we figger you're lyin'. Now you take off them fancy duds and let's see you strut around naked as a jaybird. Then we'll know if you're Buffalo Bill or Jim Bridger or maybe even Kit Carson."

One of the others snickered and said, "We'll know if he's a man or a bearded woman. I'll bet that's what he is, the bearded woman who got away from Buffalo Bill's Wild West Show."

It made me mad, the three of them stacking the deck against the old boy. Nobody in the room but me seemed to be paying any attention to what was going on. Even the bartender was looking the other way. It was plain that nobody wanted to tangle with the three hardcases.

I don't know that I wanted to, either, but I was mad enough to start toward them whether it was any of my put-in or not, or whether I'd wind up in the same shape the old man was. I was wearing my gun which I didn't always do. Not that I had any real use for it. I guess it was part of the game trying to make sure everybody took me for a man. Anyhow, this was one time I was glad I had it.

Deuce was pressed against the bar as tight as he could get, his eyes darting from one of the hardcases to the other. He reminded me of a gaunt old buck who'd just gone through a hard winter. Now he was at bay and looking for a way out, but there wasn't any.

I started to draw my gun, aiming to tell the hardcases to drag it, but I only had it half out of leather when Deuce exploded, yanking his knife out of the scabbard so fast I couldn't believe what I saw. The hardcases weren't figuring on him putting up any fight and he caught them, as the saying goes, with their pants down.

Deuce opened up that big hardcase like you'd open up

a can of beans. The tip of his knife went into the fellow's belly just above the crotch and he brought it right up to his ribs, laying his guts out for any man to see. The hardcase bellowed like a downed bull and put his hands to his belly trying to hold his innards where they belonged.

The other two went after Deuce then. I guess they'd have killed him if I'd stayed out of the row. One grabbed him and jammed his head and shoulders back over the bar while the second one hammered him in the belly with his fists.

No man could have lasted long under that kind of punishment, but before they did any real damage, I cracked the first one over the head with my gun barrel and knocked him cold. The second one whirled on me to see what had happened. I jammed my gun into his gut and said, "Make another move, mister, and you'll be trying to digest some lead."

He didn't make the move. His face turned a funny color, kind of a pasty green. "I ain't moving," he said. "Just pull that iron back far enough for me to get a breath, will you?"

I obliged. Somebody went for the doctor and somebody else called the marshal. The big man was screaming bloody murder. The one on the floor wasn't moving. The third one who had my gun in his belly was frozen solid. Deuce wiped a hand across his mouth, looked the situation over, and yelled, "Barkeep, this calls for a drink."

That's the way he was. A minute ago he was about to get killed, but now he wanted a drink. The barkeep obliged. I didn't relax my pressure with the gun much, but Deuce put the glass in my hand and I had my drink, then he said, "Thank you kindly, friend. You saved my wrinkled old hide. I never was good enough to take three men."

The doc came in a little later and got the big man on a stretcher and had him lugged across the street to his office. Then the marshal came in and asked a few questions, mostly of the fellow I had pinned against the bar. I jammed the muzzle of my gun harder than ever against the man's belly button. I guess I just about pushed it through his backbone. Right off he volunteered the information about the stolen horses.

I figured the thief would rather go to jail than have a bullet in his guts, and, judging from the way I was acting, he must have figured that was going to happen. Anyhow, the marshal hauled him and the one on the floor off to jail and said he didn't have anything on me or Deuce to hold us.

As soon as he was gone, Deuce held out his hand and said, "I'm Deuce Taylor from here and there and a little bit of yonder, and glad to be alive."

"I'm Rick Patterson," I said.

"This ruckus has sure kicked my tapeworm loose," Deuce said. "I tell you what I'll do. If you want to saunter over to the dining room with me, I'll buy you the best and biggest Goddamned steak they've got in the place."

That was exactly what he did.

3

AFTER WE FINISHED eating we went upstairs to my room and talked until midnight. By the time he left, I knew a great deal about Deuce Taylor. He was broke and buying that steak dinner was about the last thing he should have done.

He was living in a shack on the bank of the Yellowstone north of town, and he admitted he had been cadging drinks and begging meals and working everybody he could. He didn't try to operate that way with me because he figured he owed me his life, so he took almost every cent he had in his pocket to pay for the steak dinner.

He'd been up against it for quite a while, he told me. In the past he'd done about all the things it was possible for a man to do in the West, but he'd never made a big stake and he reckoned he'd have gambled it away if he had. He was an old man—I couldn't tell just how old because I wasn't sure how much he was lying, but I figured he must be at least seventy—and the things he could do best weren't in demand anymore.

The army didn't need scouts. There weren't any buffaloes to hunt, not even any bones to pick up. He was too old for cowboying and no ranch would hire him. There hadn't been any gold strikes lately where a man could hit it big. No use trying to turn wolfer. Too many others had hunted wolves until there weren't enough left to make it worthwhile.

"I've just outlived my day," he said bitterly, "and that's gospel."

18

He spent most of the evening telling his adventures. According to him, they went clear back to the days of the old mountain men and he claimed to have known person- ally men like Kit Carson, Jim Bridger, Broken Hand Fitzpatrick, the Sublettes, and all the others.

Some of this was true, I figured, but I sure couldn't swallow all of it. I didn't call him a liar, though, partly because he told a damned good story and partly because he had an unusual dignity about him and I didn't have the heart to cut him down to size. I knew it had hurt his dignity to be jumped by the hardcases the way he had in the hotel bar. I gathered it was the first time it had ever happened to him. They had taken him for a fraud, an easy mark.

"I've seen it happen before," he said. "To other old men who'd got to the end of the line. Might happen to a kid who starts bragging or a greenhorn, but I sure never figured it would happen to me. I was just standing there at the bar, you know, having a drink and not doing anything to bring those ornery boogers down on me."

I'd never met anyone like him. He was a crazy mixture. Some ways he was honest, other ways he was the greatest liar I ever ran into. He was a bum, conning everybody into giving him a living that he could, but he was strong and active enough to do the menial jobs that have to be done even in a frontier town like Miles City. The trouble was he didn't aim to take anything as low as swamping out a saloon or forking horse manure in a stable. I was impatient with him on that score because I'd taken jobs like those just to have something to eat and I'd do it again if I had to.

I knew he was claiming adventures that had belonged to someone else. Of course he always told them so he was the hero. I'd never had any time for liars, but I couldn't get mad at Deuce like I had other men I'd run into who tried to impress me with their lies. I saw through him but I didn't resent him and I wasn't sure why.

The trouble with most men like this, men I'd always classified as blowhards, was that they were bores. They couldn't tell a good story. They would repeat the same stories over and over until you were ready to scream or just walk off and leave them talking. In my judgment they were cowards, so they told these stories to make heroes out of themselves. They may even have told their yarns so often that they got to believing them.

Deuce didn't fit the pattern. I liked him. In all the months I rode and lived with him I kept on liking him. Right up until the end I could never distinguish between a lie and the truth, or whether there was some element of truth in the tale and he simply embroidered it to make a good story.

The point is, and this is where he didn't fit the pattern, he was never a bore. Too, I knew from what had happened in the bar that he was not a coward. I was convinced that he really had lived the life he talked about, that he did know how to live off the country, that he had done it many times and could do it again.

When he finally got talked out and got up to leave, I said, "Deuce, how'd you like to throw in with me?"

For a while he stood motionless staring at me in the lamplight, not saying a word, his Adam's apple bobbing up and down, then he said, "Rick, you saved my life tonight at risk of your own. Damned if I want to take advantage of you."

He was honest with me where I figured he wouldn't be honest with any other man. I said, "All right, you'll take advantage of me, but maybe I'll be doing some of the same. I'm no great prize. I figure you can teach me a few tricks that I need to know."

He looked down at the toes of his moccasins. He said, "Maybe I can at that, but I'm broke. You know that. I can't see where you'll get your investment back."

I couldn't, either. Not right then. I wasn't going to give the idea up, though. I had a hunch and I was bound to play it out. I said, "There's a lot of wilderness left in this country. Let's go look for it."

I didn't have the foggiest notion what we'd do. I was talking crazy, maybe, but I guess I was tired of swamping out saloons and forking horse manure and risking my life floating logs down a swollen river just to make profit for another man.

By nature I was a loner, but I didn't have the tools to live the kind of life I wanted to, free as the wind and being beholden to no man. I wasn't getting those tools, either, doing the kind of hang dog jobs I had been doing just to live. Maybe I'd never be able to live that kind of a life; maybe I was born too late and that life was gone just as Deuce Taylor's place in the world was gone, but I had to find out.

I have a suspicion that none of this makes sense. I've thought about it often enough, knowing that on the face of it I was going out on a limb and offering myself to be taken by an old man who, by his own admission, was a plain beggar. But it was a hunch, and I have never had a hunch like that go wrong.

Well, he stood there for a full minute I guess, then he raised his gaze to my face and he said, "By God, Rick, it's been a long time since anybody made an offer to me like that." He held out his hand. "Partners?"

"Partners," I said.

After he left I went to bed and lay there staring into the darkness and thinking about what we'd do. I knew he didn't have an outfit. He'd sold everything he owned except his clothes, his knife, his revolver, and a Winchester he had in his shack. By the time I bought him an outfit and we laid in a supply of grub and ammunition, I'd be broke. I had a lot of second thoughts right then, but I wasn't going to back out of the deal.

The next day I bought Deuce a horse, a sorrel that was far from young, but he wasn't a broken down old nag, either. He wasn't as good an animal as my buckskin, but he was all I could afford, and Deuce seemed satisfied. We hunted around Miles City until we found a cheap but serviceable saddle. I bought a few other odds and ends, picked up a pack horse the second day and enough grub to keep us going for several weeks if we had any luck hunting.

I still didn't know where we'd go and Deuce hadn't offered any suggestions. Then lightning hit, one of those deals that comes along that you have no logical right to expect. It was so perfect we couldn't think of turning it down.

A greenhorn had come in on the Dakota Belle a few days before named Al Swan. I'd seen him in the hotel lobby and it seemed like we kept running into him when we were looking for Deuce's outfit. He was a young man dressed up the way Easterners figure they have to dress when they come out West, his duds so new and clean and shiny that they hurt me to look at them.

I hadn't thought much about him. In fact, I had ignored him because I had no respect for eastern dudes. On the second evening Deuce and I were eating supper in the hotel dining room when Swan came in, saw us, and came to our table.

"May I sit down with you gentlemen?" he asked.

As far as I was concerned he was about as welcome as a case of measles, but Deuce stood up and bowed a little as if he figured Swan was visiting royalty and motioned to an empty chair. He said, "Sit down, Mr. Swan, sit down."

He sat down and said, "Thank you." I guess I looked a little hostile. He was embarrassed and jittered around for a while, staring at me and then Deuce and finally at the ceiling. He was in his early twenties, tall, no beauty with a wide jaw and a craggy face, but he had a pleasant smile, and I had a feeling he wanted to be friendly.

I began to feel sorry for him. He was a stranger from a world I had never seen and didn't want to see. I didn't know why he wanted to come here, but it was a free country and he had a right to be here. I stuck out my hand and said, "I'm Rick Patterson."

He gave my hand a good, firm shake and relaxed. "I'm Al Swan," he said, "but I guess you know that. It's easy to spot a bird like me who got out of his nest and wandered over into a new one."

"Yeah, it's easy," I said. "We seemed to be running into each other all day."

He got red in the face and stared at the tablecloth. "As a matter of fact, I was following you around. I have something in mind and I believe you are just the men I want." He raised his gaze to Deuce's face. "You know the country pretty well, don't you, Mr. Taylor?"

"Just like the palm of my hand," Deuce said expansively. "I could draw you a map of it."

I didn't think he was lying when he said that. Then I had a feeling that maybe this was going to turn out to be the very thing I was looking for and we'd get paid for doing it. That was when I decided I was going to be very fond of Mr. Al Swan.

"I've asked around about you," Swan said apologetically, and nodded at me. "I have been told that you are a hard worker and willing to take risks." He turned to Deuce and I knew then he was the one Swan really wanted. "They tell me you're down on your luck, but that you are an expert tracker and guide. I'll have to admit because you'll find it out soon enough that I am very ignorant of the knowledge and skills that a man needs to know in this country."

"And you want to pay us to get those skills and that knowledge," I said.

"That's exactly right," he said, a little surprised, I guess, that I was out ahead of him. "I want to take an extended trip with two objects in mind. First, I want to do some hunting. I understand we can find big game not very far from here: elk, antelope, deer, bear." He paused, then his eyes lighted up as he added, "I realize the big herds of buffalo are gone, but we might be lucky enough to find some old bull that's still alive hiding in one of the river bottoms."

I knew and Deuce knew that the chance of finding an old bull buffalo in one of the river bottoms was just about zero, but I saw no sense in telling Swan, so I nodded agreement as if everything he said was true. Somebody had been pulling his leg good and hard, and I didn't feel it was my duty to set him straight. An eastern greenhorn who comes out here is fair game for any native and he ought to expect getting his leg pulled, but Swan was the typical lamb asking to be shorn.

"The second thing is pretty farfetched," Swan said, "and I won't be disappointed if it doesn't happen, but I'd like to buy a ranch out here. I know that the cattle business isn't what it used to be from the financial point of view, but it's still a great adventure and I'm convinced that it will come back. These things always run in cycles and right now it's on the down turn."

Deuce didn't know what Swan was talking about and neither did I, but I nodded agreement again and Deuce said, "That's right, Mr. Swan, that sure as hell is right. There are a lot of good spreads up these rivers. Now just where did you figure on going?"

"I want your advice," Swan said, "but I thought I'd like to go up the Tongue and maybe on as far as the Little Big Horn and back down to the Yellowstone. Maybe even try the Rosebud."

"Fine country," Deuce said enthusiastically. "Yes sir, that's the finest country God ever laid out. If you want my advice, that's exactly where I'd have said to go."

"Is it a deal then?" Swan asked. "Maybe for a month or six weeks?"

"Sure it's a deal," Deuce said, and held out his hand.

Swan took it and then shook hands with me. "I'll meet you gentlemen here in the dining room early in the morning. Say, about eight o'clock?"

"We'll be here," Deuce said.

"First thing I want you to do is to find a gentle horse for me to ride," Swan said. "I mean a real gentle one, not a horse that a cowboy would call gentle that will buck me off the minute I get on him. If that happens, the whole deal is off. I know how cowboys do and I don't intend to be made sport of."

"I savvy," Deuce said blandly. "Don't worry. We'll find just the horse for you."

"We'll need a couple of pack horses," Swan went on, "and blankets and ammunition. I have a rifle, but I didn't know how many shells to buy. We'll need food, of course, though again I don't know how much to buy because I don't know how much fresh meat we'll have. Can we do all of this in a day?"

"Give us two," I said. "We'll get your saddle animal first thing. You'd better do a little riding before we start."

"Why yes," he said. "I hadn't thought about that." He rose and said, "Good night, gentlemen."

After he left Deuce looked at me with a wicked half grin. "A fat rooster ready for the plucking. Manna sent by a good God to feed his two starving children."

"I'm all for doing a little rooster plucking," I said, "but we'd better be sure we give him a good trip so he won't think he bought a dead horse. We might get a bonus if it turns out good for him."

"Sure," Deuce said. "You bet. We'll give him the best Goddamn trip a man ever had. We'll spend the next month looking for that old bull buffler down in one of them river bottoms."

Then he threw back his head and laughed fit to kill.

4

WE'D HAD OUR breakfast before Swan came to the dining room, but we sat at the table with him and drank coffee. He was unshaven and bleary-eyed. I thought at first he'd been on a drinking spree, then decided he just wasn't used to getting up so early.

As soon as he finished eating, I said, "Let's get started, Mr. Swan. It may take some time to find the kind of saddle animal you want."

"I'll go back to my room first and shave." He still didn't move for a moment, looking first at me and then at Deuce, then he blurted, "You don't expect to get up early like this every morning, do you?"

"When we're traveling, you'll be up before we are," I said. "The ground gets downright hard before sunup."

"That it does," Deuce agreed heartily.

"I just don't see any reason to start so early," Swan said. "I'd rather . . ."

"No," Deuce said. "The morning's the best traveling time of the day."

"Best time to look for that old buffalo you want, too," I said.

"Better get your shaving done," Deuce said. "Time we were rolling.

Swan rose and left the dining room. Deuce and I sat looking at each other, Deuce shaking his head. "My God," he said. "He must have a rich pappy. I don't believe he's ever done a day's work in his life."

"We'll be wet nursing him all the way up the Tongue," I said in disgust.

Swan was back downstairs in about half an hour, freshly shaven and smelling of bay rum. He said, "All right, gentlemen, let us proceed."

It took all morning to find a saddle animal for him. I knew he wasn't fooling about wanting a gentle, gentle horse and that kind was hard to find in Miles City. By noon we finally ran across a bay mare that was at least ten years old, Deuce said. She was sound enough and certainly gentle, but so slow I groaned at the thought of traveling with her for the next month.

I rode her across the Tongue River bridge and about halfway to Fort Keogh and back to the stable. I dismounted and said, "I guess she's about what you want. At least she won't buck you off, but she's so slow she's damned near useless. Wouldn't it be better to find you a horse with a little more spirit . . . ?"

"No," he said. "It'll do fine. We're not settting out to break any speed records. We've got all summer if we need it."

"Get on and try her out," I said.

He did, climbing into the saddle about as awkwardly as a human being could. He rode away, as stiff as a ramrod and thoroughly scared. I said to Deuce, "I doubt that he's ever been on a horse in his life."

"I was thinking the same," Deuce said gloomily. "I keep asking myself why in the almighty hell he wants to make a trip like this and why he even gave a minute's time to thinking about buying a ranch."

"There's a reason," I said. "We'll know what it is before we get back."

He returned to the stable in about half an hour, a big grin of satisfaction on his face. "It's not so bad, is it, gentlemen? Yes sir, this horse will be fine."

"One thing, Mr. Swan," I said. "A horse is smarter than you give him credit for. This mare knew you were afraid of her and it makes her uneasy. If you'd been forking a horse that had more spirit, he'd have unloaded you."

"I don't intend to get on such a horse. Not ever." He

patted the mare on the neck. "I'll get along fine with this one. We'll call him King."

"Might be better to call her Queen," Deuce said.

Swan got red in the face. He nodded and said, "Yes, Queen's a better name for her." He swung around to me. "How did you know I was afraid?"

I shrugged. "Let's say I just guessed."

"Well, I'm not afraid of her now," he said.

"Deuce and me will pick up the grub and pack horses," I said. "We'll plan to leave early, day after tomorrow. I think it would be a good idea for you to ride Queen about an hour this afternoon and twice tomorrow."

"Yes," he said. "I'll do that."

We bought another pack horse and more supplies and sold the animal and grub we'd bought to Swan, making a little profit on the deal. If he smelled anything wrong about the price, he never mentioned it. Afterwards I was ashamed of myself. It was like taking advantage of a child, but Deuce wasn't ashamed.

"Nobody's gonna look out for him out here," Deuce said. "If he wants people to kowtow to him because he's got a pile of dinero, then by God he should of stayed back where he came from."

"We took advantage of him for just a few dollars," I said. "If he hits a spread he wants, somebody will take advantage of him for a whole lot of dollars."

"It's his lookout, boy," Deuce said. "It's dog eat dog and you know it."

I didn't see it that way. I didn't know much about ranch values, but I didn't intend to sit with my tongue in my mouth and let him lose a pot of money. Maybe he'd just hired us to take care of his body, but I had a feeling we ought to be responsible for his pocketbook, too. I didn't argue with Deuce, though. I'd wait until the time came.

We started out two days later, not as early as Deuce and I had intended, but earlier than Swan wanted to leave. The first hour wasn't bad, then a wind came up, pushing a load of dust at us, and for the rest of the day we were just plain miserable.

This was the beginning of my respect for Al Swan. He got his bandanna out when he saw Deuce and me do it, and covered his mouth and nose and rode with his head down. He was probably a lot more uncomfortable than we were, but he didn't complain and he didn't ask for an early stop.

Deuce was smarter than I was, knowing that it takes time for a man like Swan to get a few saddle callouses on his butt. We pulled into some cottonwoods and made camp between the river and a steep bank fifty feet high. We weren't entirely out of the wind, but it was a hell of a lot better than where we had been on the road.

It wasn't much after noon, and as slow as Queen was, we hadn't gone very far, maybe ten miles. When I saw Swan ease himself out of the saddle and stand there rubbing his backside, I knew that Deuce was calling the turn just right.

We didn't discuss our camp jobs, but I realized that Swan expected to be waited on and as long as we were getting paid to do it, I didn't object. I took care of the horses and Deuce started a fire and cooked supper. When I got back to camp, I rustled more fire wood. Supper was typical prairie fare, and I didn't think Swan could get it down because he'd been a picky eater in the hotel, but to my surprise he ate heartily.

"We'd better just spend the afternoon here," Deuce said, "and break you into riding kind of slow like. You're gonna feel like you've got the biggest bruise on your hindend you ever felt. It'll be worse for a while, then it'll get better and you'll enjoy riding."

Swan grinned weakly and said, "Maybe." He got his pipe out and filled it. He tamped the tobacco down and lit it, then he added, "I'll tell you something, my friend. It's not what I'm going to feel. I feel that way already."

"You'll get over it," Deuce said.

We sat around the fire, napping and smoking, and had supper just before dark. Then Swan began to talk, having to get it off his mind, I guess, or maybe he sensed we were curious about him being out here. Once he got started talking about himself, he acted like he couldn't stop.

It seemed that his father owned a shoe factory in Rhode Island. Since the old man had the only industry in town and since he was just naturally an overbearing bastard, he figured that giving folks jobs also gave him the right to dictate their private lives even to the kind of recreation they had and the church they attended and what the preacher was to preach.

Al's mother was a mousey woman which she had to be in order to live with the old bastard. Al had one sister who defied their father by marrying a man who worked in the shoe factory. She got exactly the kind of treatment she could expect. She was cut out of the will and her husband got fired. They packed up and moved to Oregon about as far from her father as they could get. Neither parent heard from her, but Al said he got three or four letters a year and as far as he could tell they were doing fine.

Al was younger than his sister by several years and wasn't a maverick like she was. He had always bowed to his father and had it easy till about a year ago when his resentment caught up with him. He up and got married without asking the old goat's permission. They had a hell of a row, but his father didn't want to lose his son the way he'd lost his daughter. He liked Al's wife, all right, and after their baby was born, he thought the kid was the only thing in the world of any importance.

"I'd been smoldering all year," Al said. "We'd patched things up on the surface, but I kept asking myself if I was any kind of a man and I always had to give myself the wrong answer. I kept thinking of my sister Margie out there in Salem, Oregon, living the way she wanted to and not having to trot over to Pa and ask every time she wanted to blow her nose.

Margie wrote that I could get a job out there if I wanted to make the move. I'd have to do without all the things that made life easy for me and my wife and baby, but I'd be a free man. I talked it over with my wife and we decided to jump the traces.

"I told Pa about it, not wanting to just sneak off the way Margie did. I thought he'd blow up, but he didn't. He said before I made any final decision to move, he wanted me to come out here to Wyoming or Colorado or Montana and take a hunting trip and look around to see how I liked living in the West. If I found what I wanted, and I really decided to stay in the West, he'd give me all the money I needed to buy a ranch. Well sir, that was the last thing I expected, but he must have learned a lesson from the way he had treated Margie. I'd always wanted to go on a hunting trip, so I accepted his offer."

He paused, knocked his pipe out, and filled it again. Then he said, "Gentlemen, that's why I'm here, and it's why I've done some talking about buying a ranch. A poor investment, I suppose, for a man like me who knows less than nothing about the cattle business, but I can learn. I'll need some good men to help me, but I believe they can be hired.

The wind had died down and the night wasn't hot, just comfortably warm. Swan lay on his back and stared at the velvety sky, almost black now with the stars coming out, then he hoisted himself up on one elbow and looked at Deuce and me hunkered on the other side of the fire.

"You men have lived all your lives in this country," he said. "It's your world and I assume you have never been in another place that you could call a completely different world. That right?" I nodded and he took Deuce's silence for assent. "I want to tell you that this is a different world from what I'm used to. I hope I measure up. I'll do my best and I want to thank you for being patient with me."

I respected Al Swan a lot more after that. I'd never been around men like him or on a trip like this before, but I'd heard plenty about the dudes who came west and expected to be treated the way they had been in the East and made life hell for everybody around them. Well, Al Swan just didn't fit the picture. He struck me as being a decent, humble man who was trying and I gave him a lot of credit.

Deuce did, too. Later, when we walked away from the fire to take a look at the horses, he said, "I've been around plenty of men like Swan, but he's the first one I ever heard admit he didn't know his ass from a hole in the ground."

"He's all right," I said. "I like him."

"Yes sir," Deuce agreed. "He'll assay out mighty high grade."

5

Swan was all thumbs; he was downright ignorant of knowledge and skills that seemed to me a child should know, but he was willing to learn and not afraid to show his ignorance. By the end of the week he was taking care of his mare and even helped me rustle wood for the campfire.

He had brought a .30-.30 from home, but he had never done much shooting and he couldn't hit the ground when he pointed his rifle at it, so Deuce set out to teach him to shoot. By the end of that first week he was good enough to bring down his first antelope.

Judging from the way he acted, you'd have thought he had done something that was earth shaking. I guess he said half a dozen times, "Pa would never believe I did it." The meat was tougher than shoe leather, but Swan chewed away and pronounced it good.

The first day the sun and wind burned his face. We had some cloudy days and hit a couple of hard rains, but most of the time the old sun was boring right down on us. It took more than a week for the skin on his face to peel off, and even though he didn't grumble or complain, I knew damned well his face was giving him fits.

By the end of the week, he was over the worst of it, most of the deep-bruise feeling in his hindend had disappeared, and we could tell he was beginning to feel proud of himself and was enjoying the trip.

For the first few days the river was in a canyon much of the time, or at least had high banks. The grass was only

fair, and what grass there was had more than its share of
sage. Tall spurs ran down from the mountains and now
and then a rocky butte would come into view to the east.
Occasionally we'd see a scattering of pines and a few
cottonwood groves along the river, but most of the trees
were black ash and box elder.

We passed a few ranches, and the ones we did see were
road ranches whose owners made a living from people
who went by, or they were run down outfits with dowdy
women and dirty kids and a small herd of skinny cattle.

"I expected to see more ranches," Swan said. "How do
you account for so few?"

"We'll hit some good spreads farther south," Deuce
said. "This just ain't the best ranch country in the world.
The grass is thin and water's hard to get."

"There's some grass and it's not overgrazed," Swan
said. "The river's here. Plenty of water in it."

"You're right on both counts," Deuce agreed, "and I
reckon someday when the good land is all taken we'll see
some ranches trying to make it along here, but the grass is
thin." He jerked a thumb toward the Tongue. "The thing
that's bad is the deep cut banks of the river. There ain't
no water of consequence running down from the mountains. If you had a spread here, you'd have water but no
way your cattle could get to it."

That satisfied Swan, but he was plainly disappointed
not to find good ranches. I had never seen country quite
like this. I wouldn't have lived here if you'd given me the
whole kit and caboodle, but it was facinating with its red
and brown coloring. Sort of depressing, too.

One evening Deuce shot a goose. The next day Swan
brought down a white-tailed buck. He was beside himself
and said over and over, "I shot a deer. By golly, I got a
buck." The meat was better than the antelope, and it was
a relief to have an ample supply of camp meat.

Later we came into a fine grass country and Swan
found the good ranches he had been looking for. Off to the
west we saw a high, jagged ridge with some rough peaks
poling skyward. They were forty-fifty miles away, I

judged. The Big Horns, Deuce said, and a mighty rough piece of country. I could believe it.

There was so much game that Swan nearly lost his mind. He wanted to shoot every white-tailed deer we saw, but Deuce got the idea through his head that it wasn't the sporting thing to kill an animal and waste the meat. A few days later we were running low, so Deuce let him shoot another buck. We made a pretense of working through some of timber along the river and looking for buffalo sign. Of course we didn't find any, but the effort satisfied Swan.

We had been on the trail about two weeks when a storm rolled up over the mountains and headed toward us. We'd been hearing the thunder, and now the lightning was slashing across the sky that had turned a strange purple.

Swan was scared. I'll admit that it looked like the grandpappy of all thunder storms to me and I got uneasy. A ranch house was directly ahead of us. We hadn't put up at any of the ranches because we'd had no need to and Swan said he had come here to rough it.

He hadn't shaved for the two weeks we'd been gone from Miles City. Every night he'd scratch his beard and say his wife wouldn't let him come within ten feet of her if he let his beard grow that way when he was home.

"We'll hit for that ranch," Deuce said. "You've been wanting to see one. Maybe it's for sale."

Swan got his old mare going as fast as she could, but at that we didn't much more than beat the storm. The rancher met us in front of his barn and shook hands all around, saying his name was Ted Holmes. He was a lanky, lantern-jawed man, tough and strong, with the capable look that a rancher had to have in an isolated country like this. He helped us take care of our horses, then we lit out for the house. We hadn't any more than got through the door when the storm hit.

It's impossible to describe a storm like that one. The thunder was blasting away so you couldn't hear if someone tried to talk to you, and the lightning was slashing straight down toward the ground. I swear I could smell the sulphur. It hit a pine tree in front of the house and seemed to explode like a shell from a cannon and left the tree smoldering.

The rain scared me more than the lightning. I think a man would have drowned in it. I guess two or more inches must have fallen in a few minutes. I had the impression it wasn't coming in drops, but was a solid column of water pouring from the sky. A dry gulch west of the buildings was filled with muddy water within a matter of minutes and began running over its banks.

Ted Holmes stood at the window beside me, his hands jammed into his pockets. He said angrily, "I'll get some drowned steers out of this more'n likely. Looks like God just upset a bucket."

The storm moved on in a few minutes, but they were long minutes. When the thunder eased up so we could talk, Deuce said, "Well, Mr. Swan, you've got the answer to the question you asked a day or so ago."

"I've asked a lot of questions," Swan said. "Which one are you thinking about?"

"Why they build ranch buildings on top of dry ridges where there isn't any shade instead of down in the valleys among the cottonwoods," Deuce said. "You might go five, maybe ten years and not have a storm like this and be safe and sound, but sooner or later you're gonna get a gully washer. When you do, you'll lose everything you've got including your lives if you ain't had warning to get on some high ground."

Swan was staring at the brown water that had spilled out over the bank of the gulch and was licking at the barn and other outbuildings. "I've got the answer, all right," he said. "Strange thing about nature, good and beautiful until she goes on a rampage like this."

"That's right," Holmes said. "We've seen it both ways."

Mrs. Holmes had been taking care of the children in the kitchen. Now that the storm had moved on, she came into the front room with the children, and her husband introduced us. They were in their middle thirties, I guessed. They had a boy seven or eight and a girl maybe four.

The girl was the scared one. She was still moaning from fright and her mother brought them into the front room with her. Her father picked her up and comforted her, and in a minute or two she quieted down.

Mrs. Holmes wasn't what I'd call beautiful, but she was a very attractive woman, blond and blue-eyed, about five feet three or four inches, and had a fine figure. I noticed immediately that she was clean, the children were clean, and the room looked as if it had recently been scrubbed and dusted.

A huge stone fireplace took up most of one wall. A few magazines, newspapers, and a Montgomery Ward catalog were on a claw-footed stand in the middle of the room, and a bookcase filled with books stood against the far wall. The big table, a half dozen chairs, and the couch with its bear hide covering were plainly homemade, but whoever had done the work was a skilled craftsman. The rough, unplaned boards of the floor were partly covered with braided rag rugs.

The whole room had a pleasant, warm feeling about it. I told myself that here was one of those remarkable women who could, by her presence and a few feminine touches, transform a house into something very special, a talent that few ranch women possessed.

She spotted Swan for an Easterner right away in spite of his beard and hair that needed cutting and clothes that had lost their shiny newness days ago. She asked where he was from and he said Rhode Island, then she said she was from New Jersey, that she had met her husband when he was east on business and fallen in love with him.

She laughed and added, "Ted wasn't really honest with me. He didn't tell me about living next to the Cheyenne reservation, but I had supposed the Indians were civilized and Christianized by now, so I guess it wouldn't have made any difference if he had told me. He didn't mention the fact that the nearest dentist and doctor was likely to be one hundred miles away. That would have made me think twice before I said yes if I had known."

"Or that we'd have a bad winter and lose most of our

cattle," Holmes added somberly. "I'd never have got you out here if I'd told you everything."

"That's right, Ted," she said. "but now I am here and I love it. I wouldn't live in New Jersey again for anything. Do you intend to stay out here in Montana, Mr. Swan?"

He shot a glance at Deuce and swallowed. "Well, I had hopes of buying a ranch," he said, "but I don't know if my wife could stand it." He glanced around the room and added, "You've performed a miracle, Mrs. Holmes."

"That she has," her husband agreed. "I'm a lucky man."

"Oh, I don't know about that," she said, smiling. "I had the feeling I was the lucky one."

"How much would you sell this place for?" Swan asked.

Here it comes, I thought. The first ranch house he's been inside of and he wants to buy the whole layout. If Holmes was one to take advantage of him, he could do it. I glanced at Deuce, wondering if this was the time I'd have to decide whether to keep my mouth shut or warn Swan.

My worry was not justified. Holmes was taken back at first by the question, then he looked at his wife and laughed. He said, "You or John D. Rockerfeller or nobody else has got the kind of money that it would take to buy this spread. We started it from scratch. We survived the big die and in another year or two I'll have as big a herd as we can manage. We've lived through some Indian scares. My children were born here. I've got too much of my blood and sweat worked into the layout to let anyone else have it. My wife's, too."

She nodded, her eyes sparkling as she looked at her husband. "That's right, Mr. Swan. This ranch is a part of us and we're a part of it. Leaving it would be like losing one of the vital organs that makes our bodies work. Maybe we're sentimental, but it's the kind of sentiment that makes life different and good."

"You could make a big profit and start somewhere else," Swan said. "I can't do that. If I own a ranch, it's got to be one that somebody else has started."

Holmes shook his head. "I won't even talk about it."

"It's not the kind of thing you can tell anyone else," Mrs. Holmes said. "We're very much in love and this is something we have done together. It's kind of like ... well, don't laugh, but it's as if the ranch had a soul of its own and there are three of us here together."

"I understand," Swan said. "I envy you."

I didn't savvy. I had never been around people who were in love and who talked about it. Besides, the idea of a ranch having a soul was beyond my comprehension. But I didn't laugh. I didn't even feel like laughing. They were the most remarkable couple I ever met in my life and I guess I felt the way Swan did. I envied them.

6

Deuce and I spent more than a month with Al Swan, one of the happiest periods of my life. I'm not entirely sure why except that I was learning, and Al was learning more than I was, and I helped him. For some reason that gave me a lot of satisfaction.

Too, I was working and making money, but at the same time living the most completely free life I had ever lived, and I was doing exactly what I wanted to do. One of the things I have had pounded into me in more recent years is the fact that a man seldom lives that way.

Swan was enjoying himself, too. His hair and beard grew longer, his clothes got dirtier, and his marksmanship improved so that he seldom missed a shot. He ate ravenously, but still remained the long drink of water we'd first seen in Miles City.

We rode across the divide to the Little Big Horn. We spent most of one day going over the scene of Custer's defeat. Swan had read more about it than I had and he loved to talk about what he'd read. Deuce had talked to several soldiers who had served with Reno or Benteen, and to some of the Cheyennes who had fought in the battle.

We rode from the site of the Indian village across the river to the scene of the actual battle and then along the rim to where Reno's command had forted up, and finally back across the stream and through the timber where Reno had been attacked and forced to retire to the bluffs where he had holed up.

"What Custer done don't make no sense," Deuce said in disgust. "Looks to me like he plain committed suicide."

"There is a rumor to that effect," Al said. "He was at the end of the line you might say. If he'd won a spectacular victory, he would have been saved, and if he got killed, he'd be out of his troubles. He was in debt, he'd made a lot of the big wigs mad at him, and he would probably have lost his command. He was no good out of the army, so what was there for him to do?"

"If he wanted to commit suicide," I said, "he could have done it without taking his men with him."

Swan nodded grimly. "You're dead right on that," he said.

We found a lot of bones. I guess the coyotes had dug into the graves. We found plenty of old shells, too, and when we wound up back on the battlefield, we dismounted and walked around and tried to imagine what it was like, the dust and the powder smoke and the screams of wounded men and the cracking of rifle fire and the Indian war whoops.

I couldn't make it come to life, but I had a spine-chilling feeling that the spirits of the dead men were all around me and were trying to tell me something about Custer. I just couldn't make sense out of what they were saying, and it finally got on my nerves so bad I ran to my horse, stepped up, and rode back to the river.

Al joined me a little later. "Kind of spooky up there," he said. Then he grinned and added, "That's the first time I've seen you get jumpy about anything."

"First time I can remember that I have," I said. "Funny feeling. All I know is I just can't stay there any longer."

He nodded, staring back up the slope at Deuce who was still poking around among the graves. He said, "I had the same feeling. Imagination, I guess."

"Mebbeso," I said, but I didn't believe it was.

We rode on down the river, and a short time later Deuce caught up with us. He said, "I dunno. You sure can't read a man's mind, especially after he's been dead as long as Custer has, but I've got a hunch he thought he could do it no matter how many Injuns there were. A lot of officers thought the same way. They never understood the Injuns and didn't give 'em enough credit. Fetterman was the same."

"That's right," Al agreed. "And another thing. In some ways Custer was a phony. He never had really fought Indians. I don't think you can count the Washita. He sure wasn't a Crook or a Miles."

We were still talking about it when we made camp along the Little Big Horn several miles below the battlefield. The next day we rode east toward the Rosebud, taking it slow and easy and enjoying ourselves. We stopped at several good-looking ranches and Al asked if they were for sale, but none were and he never made an offer. I had a feeling that after being on the Holmes spread, nothing else looked right.

We traveled down the Rosebud, finally reaching the Yellowstone where we camped about a day's ride from Miles City. After supper we were not very talkative. All of us knew that the trip was at an end and the chances were we'd never see each other again.

The whole relationship had changed. We didn't look at Al now as if he were a greenhorn. Sure, he still wasn't a man who could take care of himself under any circumstances, but he had come a long ways. I was proud of myself and I think Deuce felt the same way about himself, but more than that, Al had become a friend.

So we just sat there beside the fire with the river making its lapping noises not far away. Finally Deuce said, "Well, Rick, you still want me to tag along with you?"

He hadn't said a word about throwing in with me since we'd left Miles City and I wasn't really sure how he felt about it now. My respect for him had grown because once we got under way he was in command and he knew where to go and what to do, and he didn't have to tell any lies to prove what he was.

"Sure I do," I said.

He took his pipe out of his mouth and stared at it. "Well now, where do you want to go?"

"I dunno," I said. "You know the whole half of the continent. Where do you suggest?"

He didn't answer for quite a while. Al and I were both watching him as he knocked his pipe out, filled it, and lighted it with a burning twig from the fire. Finally he said, "This may be the wrong thing because there's bound to be trouble down there on Powder River, but I've always had a hankering to winter in the Big Horns, do a little trapping, kill ourselves a deer or an elk when we need camp meat, and just wear out the winter till spring comes."

"Sounds good," I said. "I'm not really ambitious. What I want mostly is to keep warm and dry and have enough grub to fill my belly."

"We can do that," he said. "I know where two, three old cabins are in the mountains above Grizzly and south a piece. We may have to do some work on 'em like chinking up a few holes between the logs."

"I wish I could go with you," Al said passionately. "By God, I sure do."

"What's keeping you from doing it?" I asked.

"I've got a wife and baby and I ought to be living with them," he said. "Maybe it sounds selfish, but I've put up with a lot from my old man and I don't want to alienate him completely. There's a pile of money in the family that might go to charity if I kick over the traces."

"I can savvy the wife and baby," I said, "but I don't figure the money's worth it."

"You don't have the wife and baby," he said. "If I don't perform right, I might have to go to work."

"An ugly thought," Deuce said. "Downright ugly." He puffed on his pipe a minute, then he said, "Al, I want you to pay me off in the morning. I'm not going into town with you. Rick, you'll find me right here when you come back. You buy the supplies we'll need and I'll pay you for my share after you get here day after tomorrow."

This took both me and Al back a ways. Al asked, "What's the matter with you, Deuce? It doesn't sound like you. Come on into Miles City with us tomorrow and we'll get the red paint out and paint the town up good."

"Yeah, we could do it, but I'll pass it up," Deuce said. "I'll tell you how it is. I never had nobody really trust me before. I ain't exactly truthful or honest. Fact is, I'm a mean son of a bitch and about half fake. Then Rick comes along and buys me an outfit and says he can learn something from me. I aim to take him at his word. Kind of a good feeling to know you're being trusted."

I wasn't surprised that he was half fake because I'd just about decided that myself, but I was surprised to hear Deuce admit it. Anyhow, I still couldn't put this together with what he was saying about not going to Miles City.

"I still don't savvy," I said. "What you were just saying hasn't got anything to do with riding into town with us."

"It's got everything to do with it," he said. "You see, every time I made myself a little stake, and it didn't make any difference whether I earned it, stole it, or found it, I'd always hit town and get drunk or gamble it away or spend it on some damned floozy who wasn't worth the pepper it'd take to make her sneeze. It's what I'd do this time if I got to Miles City and then you'd have to foot the bill again. I just ain't gonna do it."

"All right," I said. "You're the boss, but you're going to get mighty tired of sitting here for a couple of days by yourself and watching the Yellowstone flow by."

"It's better'n not having a river to flow by," he said, grinning. "You never know what'll go past."

I didn't figure there was any use to argue with him. Besides, he was probably right. In the morning Al paid him his wages, we packed up, then headed down the river. We didn't talk much on the way. When we got to town, we put our horses up, he paid me, then wrote out a bill of sale for the mare and the two pack horses.

"I'll give them to you," he said. "You'll need the pack horses if you're taking off with Deuce. Maybe you can get a little something for the mare." He laughed, and added, "You were right, Rick, about me getting tired of that old mare and her slow pace. I guess that if I ever do anything like this again, I'll get a better horse."

"One that might buck you off?" I asked.

"One that might buck me off," he agreed, "and I

remember telling you I never wanted to fork a horse that might." He rubbed his back side and the inside of his thighs, and went on. "You know, I ought to buy me a horse when I get home and keep riding, or I'll lose my callouses."

"No reason why you couldn't," I said.

We walked to the depot and Al found out that there was an eastbound train going through Miles City at nine that evening, so he bought a ticket, invited me to have dinner with him in the McQueen House, and then asked me to walk back to the depot.

"I'm going to keep my beard and hair long till I get home," he said, "and I'll wear the same clothes. I'm keeping that one fine set of antlers, but I suppose nobody will believe me when I say I shot the buck. I'll have to shave my beard and change clothes within five minutes after I walk into the house, but I want my wife to see the way I look."

"What about your pa?" I asked.

He shot me a quick glance and nodded. "Sure, I know what you mean. You're right. I'm still a long ways from being a free man. Maybe I never will be, but I won't let Pa see me looking like this."

"Break it off with him, Al," I said. "You could make it out here. When I first met you, I didn't think there was a chance, but you're not the same man you were when we rode out of Miles City."

"No, I'm not," he said. "Maybe I will break it off some time. I'm not ready yet." He dug a piece of paper and a pencil stub out of his pocket. He wrote his name and address on it and handed it to me. "Maybe you'll need it someday. If you settle down so I can write to you, let me hear from you."

"I will," I said.

We heard the train whistle a few blocks away. He held out his hand and I shook it. He said, "Rick, I can't tell you how much this trip . . ."

Then the corners of his mouth began to quiver and he couldn't say another word. He wheeled away and strode along the track, not looking back at me. The train pulled in and he stepped aboard, but I didn't see him until the last car passed me. He waved from the rear platform. I waved back. I didn't think I'd ever see him again, but I was dead wrong on that.

7

THE NEXT MORNING I sold the mare for ten dollars and felt lucky to get that much. I laid in only enough supplies to last for a few days because I figured we'd do as well in Wyoming and there didn't seem to be any use toting our stuff all that way when it wasn't necessary.

Still, it took most of the morning to do all of that along with saddling my sorrel and loading one pack animal with the grub I bought. I didn't buy any traps, figuring we could do that in Wyoming, too. I rode hard the rest of the day, but I didn't get back to Deuce until dark.

"Figured you'd got your dinero and lit out for the Black Hills," Deuce grumbled. "What the hell you been doing all this time?"

I didn't want an argument, thinking he was grumpy because he'd been alone for two days, so I didn't flare up but just told him what I'd been doing. I'd bought one bottle of whisky in Miles City. He brightened up when he saw it. After he'd had a couple of swigs from the bottle, he was his usual cheerful self.

We sat by the fire after supper and smoked. Deuce wanted to know all about me leaving Swan. He nodded after I told him, and said, "If I don't miss my guess, he'll be out here in another year or so. Never seen a greenhorn change the way he did. Never thought he would when we rode out of Miles City with him."

We pulled out at dawn, heading south along the Rose-bud, then angled west. We weren't in any hurry because we had several weeks of good weather before we'd see any

47

snow, so we had plenty of time to find our cabin and get set for winter.

When we reached Grizzly, we put our horses up in a livery stable and took a room in the Big Horn Hotel. Before we left to go down to the dining room, I asked, "What did you mean that night we were camped on the Yellowstone before Al left and you said there'd be trouble on Powder River?"

"Reckon I shouldn't have said it," he muttered. "It won't hurt us none. Hell, we'll be in the mountains a long ways from Powder River."

"I want to know," I said sharply, irritated by the way he was trying to duck my question.

"It's the same old story you've heard a dozen times in the West," he said. "There's a bunch of settlers in Smith County, little fellers that took up a quarter section and run a shirttailful of cows. Maybe they brand a few mavericks which you ain't supposed to do in Wyoming. Maybe they even steal a few head from the big outfits. Anyhow, the big cowmen started talking about putting a stop to it by cleaning out all the little fry they call rustlers. Just talk, I reckon, seeing as that's all it's been so far."

He was right about it being an old story in the West, but I knew it was worse in Wyoming because the Cattlemen's Association had a big hand in politics. They seemed to control the legislature and get any law passed they wanted.

Some of the cowmen had even lynched a man and woman down on the Sweetwater a year or so ago and nobody had gone to jail as far as I knew. In other words, if you're a cattleman with enough wealth and power, you can murder all you want to and not be touched by the law. A hell of a situation, I thought, but at that time I didn't know the half of it.

We went downstairs for supper. I kept thinking about it, and after we were done eating and just sitting there waiting to finish our coffee, I asked, "What's the law like here in Smith County?"

"It's all right now," he said. "That's why I don't figure anything but smoke will come out of all this fire. They had a bastard for sheriff a while back, a regular old style gunman killer named Pete Martin. The big outfits put him in and figured they was safe as long as he packed the star, but by the time the next election came around, enough settlers had moved in to elect their own man, so they beat Martin. I don't think he's even in the county anymore."

"Who's sheriff now?"

"Feller who owns a little spread on Crystal Creek below town," Deuce said. "Name's Pinky Benson. Good man."

We left the hotel and made a round trip on Main Street. The business district was good sized for a small cow town, so I figured there must be a pretty good settlement in the county. Crystal Creek bisected the business block, a beautiful, clear stream that made me think a man could catch a fair-sized trout right here in town. It was spanned by a bridge with a heavy plank floor. You could hear a horse crossing it a long ways off because his hoofs hit the planks with pistol-like sharpness that seemed to echo all up and down the street.

We met several men who knew Deuce. They always stopped and shook hands warmly and seemed glad to see him. He introduced me and then they shook hands with me. I got the feeling that Deuce had been well liked here. He never had said how long he'd lived in Smith County or what he'd done to make a living while he was here and I hadn't quizzed him about it, but it was plain he was pretty well-known.

When we got back to the hotel, we stepped into the bar for a drink before we went to bed. The barkeep and the townsmen who were there were greeting Deuce with enthusiasm. He introduced me again and I got a little ribbing about throwing in with Deuce.

"He'll steal your eye teeth," one man said. "You watch him, boy."

"And always walk behind him," another man said. "He's damned good with that knife of his. Why, one time I seen him pin a fly to the wall yonder. He got one wing with his knife, then he borrowed another knife and pinned the other wing as slick as a whistle."

"Shut up, you swiveled-tongued liars," Deuce said angrily. "Rick here might believe you."

They slapped him on the back and said they didn't figure I would. Deuce called for a drink for us and the barkeep sized him up, careful like, and asked, "You gonna pay for 'em?"

"You're Goddamned right I'm gonna pay for 'em," Deuce said hotly.

"All right, then you'd better have the money," the bartender said, and poured the drinks.

I wasn't quite sure then how Deuce had got along here or what he'd done for a living. They seemed to like him, all right, but then I guess folks in Miles City had liked him, too. Maybe he'd been living off other people in Grizzly the same way he had been there.

When we went back to our room, Deuce was still fuming. "Damned bastard," he said. "That bartender had no business acting as if I might not pay for the drinks."

"He knew you," I said. "He must have had some reason for acting the way he did."

"Sure he knew me," Deuce snapped. "I lived in Smith County three years. I worked when I was here, too. I was roundup cook. I . . ."

He stopped and looked at me. I don't know what he saw in my eyes. Doubt, maybe, because I was sure having them right then. He sat down on the bed and ran a hand across his face. He took a long breath that sounded almost like a sob.

"I shouldn't have come back here," he said in a low tone. "I wanted to come back because I've got a little money in my pocket and I've got you for a partner. I wanted folks to see me this way. There was a time when the army needed scouts and wagon trains needed guides and I made out purty well, but it's more'n time I quit living in the past. I figgered I had quit about six weeks ago when you turned up in Miles City." Suddenly he slapped his leg. "By God, I have quit living in the past. You'll see, Rick."

We went to bed, but I didn't sleep for a while. Funny thing. Like Deuce, I wished we hadn't come to Smith

County. There were plenty of other places where we could have got away from people and lived in the mountains, but no, Deuce had to try to make folks forget he'd been a beggar living off his exploits of another time. Still, I had no reason to question our association. He had shown in our trip with Al Swan that he could deliver what he'd promised. I had no reason to think he wouldn't with me.

After breakfast the next morning we left the hotel and crossed the street to the big store on the bank of Crystal Creek. I hadn't noticed the name the evening before because it had been dusk, but now the tall, black letters hit me: GENERAL MERCHANDISE, B. U. JOYFUL, PROP.

"What kind of a joke is this, Deuce?" I asked. "Nobody could have a name like that."

Deuce laughed. "Looks clean loco, don't it? Well sir, far as anybody knows around here, his name really is Joyful. He came to Grizzly when it was just a collection of tents and a couple of log cabins and started a small store and saloon. Now he's got the biggest business in the county and he's well thought of." Deuce nodded at the lean-to on the far end of the building. "That's his saloon, but he claims he makes more money from his store than he does out of the saloon."

"Even if his name is Joyful," I said, "how could he come up with initials like that?"

"Maybe his parents never thought about the initials," Deuce said. "He says his names are Buchanan Ulysses, and nobody would call him by those names, so he just uses the initials."

I followed Deuce inside, expecting to see some kind of freak, and I wasn't far wrong. A man came out of the gloomy rear of the store, a very fat man who sort of rolled along. He bellowed, "Well, Deuce, I heard you were in town. Glad to see you."

He held out a huge hand and Deuce shook it, then introduced me as his partner and Joyful shook hands with me. I expected to find his grip flabby, but it wasn't. There was more strength in his fat body than I had suspected.

"We're fixing to do some trapping this winter," Deuce

said, "so we've got to lay in a supply of grub and ammunition. We'll pay, B.U. We ain't asking for credit."

"Good, good," Joyful said in his great voice. "I never for a minute expected you to ask for credit. No sir, not for one minute."

He was a fair to middling liar, too, I thought, but I didn't say so. Deuce brought the pack horses to the hitching pole in front of the store, then went back for the saddle horses. I took care of all the buying except the traps. I thought Deuce knew more about them than I did. I had the supplies piled up on the boardwalk ready for Deuce to pack by the time he brought the saddle horses. He was better at packing than I was.

It was close to noon by the time we were ready to go. We paid Joyful and shook hands with him. He asked, "Where you headed, Deuce?"

"I dunno," he answered. "We'll look around and pick out a place before snow flies." He hesitated, then asked, "When I was here before, there was a lot of talk about the big outfits sending in an army to clean out the settlers and little ranchers. Was it all wind?"

Joyful's face had been serene and happy up to that moment. As soon as Deuce asked the question, his face turned sour. "Hell no, it ain't all wind. Just a few days ago Sonny Tilden was riding home with his winter's supply of grub he'd just bought from me when he got dry gulched. His team ran away, scattering the grub all over tarnation. Now his wife is out of money, no grub and nobody to tend the stock. It's just beginning, Deuce. By God, it's just the beginning."

"Pinky ain't made no arrests?" Deuce asked.

Joyful shook his head. Deuce asked, "Well, ain't nobody got any idea who done it?"

"Nobody's got any proof," Joyful said. "A couple of men saw Pete Martin riding away from where the shooting took place, but that ain't proof he done the shooting."

We stood there a minute, looking at each other. I didn't know anything about this Sonny Tilden, but just the idea of what had happened made me sick.

Finally Deuce said, "I guess we'd better ride."

We mounted and, leading the pack horses, rode south out of town. After while Deuce said, "Powder River's gonna run red with blood before this is over. I just hope we can stay out of it."

"So do I," I said.

It didn't occur to me then, but afterwards I wondered if Deuce sensed what was going to happen.

8

WE RODE SOUTH several miles before we turned west into the mountains. Deuce had three cabins in mind where he'd stayed at one time or another, but admitted it had been several years since he'd been here and something might have happened to the cabins in that time.

He was sure right about something happening to the first one. It had been burned to the ground. The grass had grown so high we had trouble finding where the cabin had been. When we did find the site, there was nothing left but a few charred logs and a rusty old stove. Deuce just stood there and cussed for about five minutes straight hand running.

"It was the damned Association that done it," he said. "I'll bet money on it. They knew some of the little fellers, rustlers they call 'em, used to come up here and stay when it got too hot for 'em along Powder River, so they burned it. I hope they fry in hell."

I thought he was jumping a long ways to make that judgment, not knowing anything about what had happened here, but I didn't argue with him. He'd made up his mind about the Association years ago and all of his sympathies were with the small ranchers, and he wasn't going to change his mind. Not that he had any reason to. It was just that he condemned the Associaion on general principles.

We had followed a narrow twisting canyon for miles. It had been slow going, so now Deuce cocked his head, took

a look at the sun, and said he allowed we'd better camp
on the creek, that it was a day's ride to the next one.

Our luck was no better the following afternoon. The
second cabin had been torn down and most of the logs
hauled away. I couldn't figure out what had happened. If
anyone wanted the logs, I suppose it was easier to come
here and tear down the cabin and haul them off than to
cut them from standing timber, but if it had been an old
cabin, the logs just wouldn't be worth hauling away.

I mentioned that to Deuce, but he shook his head. "It
was a purty new cabin and it was in right good shape the
last time I stayed in it. A homesteader built it a few years
before that, but he starved out." Deuce motioned around
the little flat. "Hell, the ground's rocky it's too high, the
weather's tough, and there ain't enough level land anyhow. He just starved out."

"Still, it looks to me as if a man would be ahead to cut
his own logs," I said.

"Depends on what he wanted 'em for," Deuce said,
scratching a cheek with one hand. "If he aimed to build
another cabin to live in, I'd say yes, but if he just wanted
it for a line cabin for summer use, this was the cheapest
and easiest way to get logs. Or maybe he wanted 'em for a
corral. Anyhow, there ain't enough left here to make it
worth working on. If we don't have better luck tomorrow,
we'll have to build us one."

Our luck turned the next day. I was glad that this was
the only one of the three that had survived. It was within
ten feet of a beautiful, clear creek that had a dozen holes
where I knew I'd find trout, and it was in the center of a
big meadow with grass up to my knees. Our horses could
make out all winter here. Lodgepole pines grew all around
the meadow. Some were dead ones that could be cut for
firewood.

The cabin itself was in good shape. A couple days'
work would take care of the chinking and another day
would clean out the inside. That was about all that was
needed. The roof was in excellent condition, and the
fireplace was a beauty. There was a bunk in one corner,

the tick needing to be stuffed with new grass, a table, and two chairs. Everything we really needed was here.

"We can't complain about this," I said.

"No, we can't," he said, and stood looking around the meadow for a good three minutes before he added, "We're taking a chance staying here on account of it belongs to the T-in-a-box, which same is the biggest spread on Powder River. If some of their hands catch us, we'll be in hot water, but from the looks of the grass, there ain't been no cows up here this summer."

"From the looks of the inside of the cabin," I said, "nobody's been in it all summer, either."

"No, that's a fact," he said, "so I think we'll be safe enough to move in. We'd better make up our minds to one thing though. If any cowhands ride in here, we'd best shoot first and ask what they're doing here later."

I didn't like the sound of that, but I didn't see any reason why the T-in-a-box cowhands would care if we wintered here. We weren't bothering their grass, and we'd leave the cabin in better shape come spring than it was now.

We went to work and had the cabin fixed in about three days. I fished a few minutes every evening and caught four or five pan-sized trout each time. We did some hunting after we were done with the cabin and I got a spike buck the first afternoon. After that we spent several days exploring the mountains around the cabin, Deuce looking for sign to see what we could catch, come winter.

"Ain't much left around here to trap," he said, "but it'll be a good place to winter anyhow. Just one thing, Rick. We're in the southern edge of the Big Horns and it's a long ways to Grizzly from here, so when we go out for supplies, we'll have to go to Jones's Store. It ain't much, but it'll have what we need."

"Who's Jones?" I asked.

"An old-timer," he said. "A purty good old man, as long as we've got the dinero to pay for what we buy. He's got three boys who run a few head of cattle and operate a freight line between Casper and Grizzly. I'm a little surprised the Association ain't burned him out and killed the boys. Old man Jones talks purty tough about the Association."

I didn't aim to worry about old man Jones and his three sons, but I did worry about Deuce. He was as jumpy as a Mexican bean, looking downstream every few minutes when he was outside, and going to the door when he was inside and standing there listening for a full thirty seconds, his head cocked, not saying a word.

"If you're going to get this boogery," I said, "we'd better move on."

"I'll be all right," he said more sharply than he needed to. "We've just got to keep watching. That's all. I don't want to be surprised. Them bastards can think of things no Sioux or Cheyenne would dream of."

As far as I was concerned, I had enough to do to keep my mind off the T-in-a-Box cow hands. I spent a good deal of time every day chopping down dead lodgepole pines, trimming them, and dragging them to the cabin, using a rope and my saddle horse. Then I had to work them up into short lengths that would fit the fireplace.

I fished as long as the weather was reasonably warm, but when it turned cold, the creek froze and that stopped my fishing. I hunted a good deal, so we always had elk meat or venison. Once I shot a black bear and Deuce helped me skin it. We had all the bear meat we could handle and a rug for the floor.

Deuce didn't calm down until we had a heavy snow in November, and then he said he didn't figure we'd be getting any visitors this late. He strung out his traps and I went with him part of the time when he checked them.

Later in December he came down sick and I had to look after the traps myself and skin anything we caught which wasn't much. He was well by the end of December and made his monthly ride to Jones's Store. This was something he always did because I didn't know where the store was and I didn't want to know. Deuce enjoyed visiting with old man Jones and his sons, but as far as I was concerned, the solitude was just right. I guess I was born a loner. Anyhow, I didn't need to see anybody else.

Sometimes Deuce got on my nerves and I wished Al

Swan was here with us. We played cards in the evening after the weather turned cold. Deuce was a sore loser. I never figured a card game was worth losing your temper over unless you had some money up, so I didn't argue. After while Deuce would run out of wind and shut up. He'd look at me and shake his head and grin a little, then he'd say, "You ain't much fun, Rick. You're too damned good-natured."

The winter was a mild one compared to what most winters in the Big Horns were, Deuce said. There were only a few times he couldn't have ridden to the store if he'd wanted to and even fewer days when we couldn't get to the traps or cut wood.

Once in March Deuce was more upset and nervous when he got back from the store than any time I'd been with him. "They shot and killed the oldest Jones boy," he blurted. "Dry gulched him when he was taking salt out to his cattle. Nobody knows who done it, but Pete Martin was seen a little ways from where the boy's body was found. He done it, all right. Now the old man's in trouble and he knows it. He's trying to sell out, but who wants to buy a death trap like his store?"

"I don't see why it should be a death trap," I said. "What difference does it make to the Association whether he has a store or not?"

"You ain't very smart if you can't figure that out," he said. "The big bastards don't want a store on Powder River. They don't need it. They freight in what they need from Casper in the fall and that lasts a year, but the little fellers like us are the ones who buy from Jones, so the Association figures his store is one thing that helps the rustlers, as the Association calls 'em, to stay on Powder River."

After that it was only a question of days until we'd move on. Every day Deuce got a little jumpier. I don't think he ever slept more than half an hour at a time. We'd done about all the trapping we were going to do, and we were running low on grub. Both of us knew we were going to have to get out and rustle some work. Maybe Deuce

would go back to panhandling, but for me it was going to
be a job.

Deuce made one more trip to the Jones's Store. He was
a mess when he got back with a bloody nose, a black eye,
and a swollen lip. "They done it just like I knowed they
would," he snarled. "By God, they burned the store and
all the other buildings to the ground. I didn't figure out
what happened to Jones and his wife and his sons."

"How'd you get into trouble?" I asked.

"I didn't have to work at it," he said. "I was kicking
around in the ashes thinking I'd find some bones when
three T-in-a-Box riders showed up and worked me over.
They recognized me and wanted to know what I was
doing there. I said I was trapping in the mountains and
came down for supplies. They said I had twenty-four
hours to get out of the country and they'd hang me if they
found me there after that."

"What'd you do to get a beating?" I asked. "You must
have done something to make them mad."

"Yeah, I did," he said and looked away. "It was my
own fault. I was so damned mad I cussed 'em good and
told 'em I figured they was the ones who murdered old
man Jones and his family. If I'd just ridden off, they
would have let me go, chances are. Now they probably
will hang me if they run into me again."

I had no way of knowing whether they had meant it or
were just hoorawing a scared old man, and that's what he
was. I wasn't real sure why, but he apparently thought
they meant it. Or maybe it was the worry he'd had all
winter about staying here. Anyhow, it was plain we'd best
be moving. It was time we were breaking up, too. I had
learned all I could from him, we were almost broke and I
had no intention of supporting him.

We'd get a few dollars from our pelts and maybe we'd
sell our pack animals. After that we'd go our separate
ways. Sometimes I had a feeling Deuce would have a
better disposition if he could work up a good ruckus with
me and get rid of the steam that was bottled up in him,
but I wasn't built that way. I liked to fight, but not with a
friend.

We packed up and started out before sunup. The morning was clear and warm, but in the afternoon clouds rolled down from the peaks and snow began to fall. The temperature must have dropped thirty degrees or more in a couple of hours. We were out of the mountains then and riding along the rim of the valley.

"We're gonna have to hole up somewhere," Deuce said. "I've seen some spring storms that were lollapaloozas and would freeze a man to death."

It was dusk then, but I'd spotted a small spread on the river. I said, "Let's get down to Powder River, Deuce. There's a ranch yonder. Maybe we can stay there."

He didn't answer for a minute, then he said, "I dunno who's living there. That place used to be the Circle A, but it was another brand that belonged to Chill Arthur who had the biggest spread in these parts. He died just after I left the country, so I dunno whether his outfit broke up into several little places or someone took the whole layout over. If them T-in-a-Box riders are there, I'm in trouble."

"They don't know me," I said. "I'll go down and holler and we'll find out who's staying there."

"All right," he said reluctantly. "I'll stay back a piece, but close enough to see who's there when you call to 'em. If I recognize 'em and know they're men we can trust, I'll ride on in." He paused, then added hopefully, "Could be some small fry. They're sure taking all the range they can. That's why T-in-a-Box is so damned ornery."

"Come along," I said. "We'll soon know."

We headed down off the rim, with me taking the lead. It was almost dark when we reached the buildings. Deuce stopped by the barn and I rode on to the cabin. I began to wonder how stupid I was. The way things were shaping up, I figured that whoever was inside would likely start shooting the minute I hollered. But I was out in the open and I couldn't back out now.

"Hello the house," I yelled.

Then my heart began to pound as I waited, not knowing whether I'd get a friendly word or a bullet.

9

I'M SURE IT was only a few seconds that I sat my saddle as I waited for an answer, my skin crawling all over me. I expected a bullet, but none came. It seemed an eternity before the light went out, the door banged open, and a man called, "Who is it?"

I couldn't make out what he looked like, but I saw him move through the door fast. Then he stood with his back to the wall of the cabin, a gun in his hand. I was afraid he couldn't see me well enough to know that I wasn't holding my gun.

"The name's Rick Patterson," I said. "My partner's back there apiece. We're looking for a place to spend the night."

"Who's your partner?" the man asked.

"Me," Deuce called, and rode into sight. "That voice couldn't belong to nobody but Matt Coleman. How the hell are you?"

"Deuce," the man yelled. "By God, it's Deuce Taylor. What are you doing down here, you no good old hoss thief?"

"You be careful how you talk in front of my partner," Deuce said amiably. "He's half man, half cougar, and he'll eat you alive if he takes a notion to. He looks out for me real good."

"Bert, come out here," Coleman bellowed. "Who do you suppose blew in with this wind?"

A second man stepped outside. "Come on in, Deuce," he said. "All kinds of tumbleweeds blow around in these

April winds. We've got enough slow elk and beans for supper."

"You mean T-in-a-Box elk, don't you?" Deuce asked.

"Well, I guess them sons of bitches have eaten enough Circle A meat that we won't never get ahead of 'em," Coleman said. "Keep your eye on them steaks, Bert. I'll give these drifters a hand with their horses."

He was a big man, and the closer he got to me the bigger he looked. I'd heard of Matt Coleman when I'd been in Montana, though I doubt that he'd ever been north of Wyoming. He was one of those legendary cowboys who had grown up in Texas, came north with the big herds, and had worked for years as foreman on several big Wyoming spreads. His feats using a rope and breaking horses were talked about all over the cattle country. I guess his fighting, drinking, and screwing abilities were just as famous.

Deuce introduced us. I shook hands with Coleman and wondered if I'd ever be able to use my hand again. He thumped Deuce on the back, called him a wandering old fraud, and asked what he was doing here and where had he been.

"I've been all over the country," Deuce said. "I was in Miles City when I ran into Rick here. He wanted to get away from people for a winter, so we came down here an we've been trapping in the mountains."

"Get anything?" Coleman asked.

"Not much," Deuce answered. "Beaver mostly. We'll sell our pelts in Casper and we'll have a little drinking and eating money."

After we had taken care of our horses, we walked back to the cabin, the wind picking up and coating our backs with snow before we reached the front door. I hadn't realized how cold and wet I was until I got inside and shut the door, then I began to shiver. I pulled off my hat and sheepskin and stood by the fireplace, my hands out.

Deuce shook hands with the other man and they pounded each other on the back, then Deuce introduced me to Bert Springer, a banty of a man about half Matt Coleman's size.

"Glad to meet you, boy," Springer said. "You look like you might be good for something. How'd you happen to team up with a no-good old goat like Deuce here?"

This was supposed to be good-natured hoorawing, but it irritated me. I said, "I found out he's good for a lot of things, Mr. Springer."

"Well, he always was a hard drinking old bastard," Coleman said from where he stood at the stove. "You know anything else he does good?"

"Yes sir," I said. "I saw him cut a man open in Miles City so you could see his backbone by looking at his belly button. A man about your size, Mr. Coleman."

"That a fact, Deuce?" Coleman asked.

"That's a fact," Deuce said. "Trouble was he had two friends. If it hadn't been for Rick here, they'd have finished me."

"I always knew you'd amount to something," Coleman said. "Just took time, I guess."

Deuce laughed. "A hell of a long time."

"Pull up a chair," Coleman said. "The meat's done, the coffee's hot, and the biscuits are ready to eat."

There wasn't much variety to the meal, but it tasted good and there was plenty of it. After we finished, we lighted our pipes. Springer threw more wood into the fireplace, and Deuce and I did the dishes.

"You heard about the Jones boy?" Deuce asked.

"Sure did," Coleman answered. "Pete Martin again. There's been a warrant issued for him, but he left Smith County in a hurry. I expect he's down in Cheyenne with all them rich nabobs who hired him. If he ever shows his ugly face in Smith County again, he's a dead man."

"What happened to the rest of the Jones family?" Deuce asked.

"Some of the T-in-a-Box boys warned 'em to leave," Coleman said, "but Jones always has been a stubborn old boy, so he stayed. The next day his visitors came back, started Jones and his wife toward Grizzly, and burned his buildings. The same bunch caught the two boys with their freight wagons south of here apiece, shot the horses, burned the wagons, and made the boys head back to Casper on foot."

"The Cheyenne newspapers talk about the reign of terror in Smith County," Springer said, "and they're right, only the terror's on the other side. Ain't none of us they call rustlers who can ride to Grizzly and not expect to get murdered on the way."

"Only a question of time till we'll have a civil war," Coleman said bitterly. "I think we're going to have to organize and run every cowman out of Smith County who's got more'n a hundred cows under his iron."

"If we don't, they'll run us out," Springer said, "which same is what they're trying to do."

"I used to hear talk about a list of men they were gonna hang as rustlers," Deuce said. "Fixing to send in a big bunch of armed men and clean out the county. What about it?"

"There's more talk than there used to be," Coleman said, "and it's getting hotter. There is such a list all right, and my name is the first one on it. Bert's on it, too. It'll come, maybe sooner than we expect."

"If they do something like that," Springer said, "they'll stick their noses into a hornet's nest. It'll be like it was back in the revolution when the minutemen rose up against the redcoats."

"That's right," Coleman said. "We've had too many murders. Too many burnings like the Jones's Store. We're having a meeting next Sunday in Grizzly. I don't know just what we'll do, but I'm aiming to argue that we need a patrol along the south edge of the county to stop any man from coming in who's a stranger and looks like a gun-man."

"I keep telling him it won't work," Springer said. "The county's too big. You can't keep a man out who wants to come in."

We sat there, nobody saying a word, but I could sure feel the wild fury that had built up in Coleman and Springer. Finally Coleman said, "A bunch of 'em tried to kill me last year, you know. Busted into my cabin on Buffalo Creek, aiming to shoot me in bed, but I wasn't asleep. I had my hand on my gun and I started spraying lead when they rushed in." He laughed sourly. "You should have seen 'em rush back out."

"It ain't just that they're really after rustlers," Springer said. "Most of us used to work for 'em till they fired us. After the Big Die they didn't need so many hands 'cause their herds were cut down. What did they expect us to do, starve to death?"

"I reckon they did," Coleman said, "but it might have been cheaper for 'em if they'd kept us on the payroll. They've had some cattle stole, all right, but most of us who are trying to get started with a little spread of our own ain't the ones who are doing the stealing. They never try to find out who's guilty. They want all of us off the range, so they paint everybody who don't belong to the Association with the same brush."

"They've got the money, so they've got the power," Springer said. "They go together and make a tough hand to beat."

"What about this Circle A?" Deuce asked. "It used to be part of Chill Arthur's holdings, but I heard he died."

"That's right," Coleman said. "His heirs all live in the East and none of 'em wanted to come out here, so his lawyer in Grizzily divided the estate up into little spreads and me'n Bert bought this one. We've got about ninety head between here and the mountains."

"The bank in Grizzly backed us," Springer added, "though I think it was mostly B.U. Joyful who put up the dinero."

"A tough old bird," Coleman said. "Don't let all that lard fool you. If it wasn't for him, the big outfits would have it all to themselves in Smith County. He's the first man they'll hang if they ever get to Grizzly." He yawned and wiped a hand across his face. "Well, there's no sense in acting like this was a wake. Get your fiddle out, Bert."

Coleman walked to the cupboard and returned with a bottle of whisky and Springer dug out his violin. I took one drink from the bottle and sprawled out on a bear hide rug in front of the fireplace. For an hour Springer played one tune after another ranging from "Darling Nelly Gray" and "Just Before the Battle, Mother" to pieces like "Shoo Fly, Don't Bother Me" and "Little Brown Jug."

Most of the time Coleman was singing with him in a first class tenor, and once in a while Deuce would chime in with a squeaky voice that was more soprano than anything else. I guess I dozed off once or twice, but most of the time I just lay there, listening and feeling completely at peace.

I don't remember ever feeling like that before or since, but I had a haunting feeling that I wished this moment would never pass, but would go on and on, that it was a period in time that was good and the future would never bring another moment as good.

It did end, of course. Coleman yawned and said they had to get up early and drive back a few steers that had wandered across Powder River. He tossed me a blanket and Deuce lay down beside me on the bear rug. I went to sleep at once. When I woke, it was still dark with not much more than a hint of dawn in the eastern sky. Deuce was gone.

Coleman was hunkered down beside the fireplace whittling shavings off a piece of pine. He asked, "You awake, kid?"

I yawned and rubbed my eyes. "Guess so," I said. "You're an early bird if I ever saw one."

"Reckon so," Coleman said. "A bunk always gets hard for me about this time of morning. I sent that partner of yours to the river to get some water, but he ain't got back. Pull on your boots and go see what's happened to him. Maybe he fell in and can't swim. The water's about a foot deep there."

I pulled on my boots, took my sheepskin and hat off the antlers by the door and put them on, then stepped outside. The wind had died down, but the snow was three or four inches deep. The sky was clear and I could see more stars than I could count, but it was cold for April.

I followed Deuce's tracks to the stable, wondering if we'd make it to Casper today. I made the turn around the corner of the stable, fixing to holler at Deuce, but I didn't make a sound. One man grabbed me and slapped a hand over my mouth and another one prodded me in the back with the muzzle of his six-shooter, saying, "One sound out of you and you'll never make another one."

I took him at his word. I couldn't have made any noise if I'd wanted to with a hand over my mouth, but then, I didn't want to. Not with that .45 poking me in the back the way it was.

10

FOR A MOMENT I was too surprised and confused to figure out what was happening. In the thin dawn light I saw that Deuce was a prisoner, too, and then I began seeing the shadowy figures of a lot of men, fifteen or twenty. About that time it hit me. These men were the invaders, the army the Association had sent into Smith County to wipe out the small ranchers they called rustlers.

The hand over my mouth was jerked away as a man moved toward me from where he had been standing in front of Deuce. He came up very close to me. He was short and pudgy with a new, stiff-brimmed Stetson.

"Who are you?" he asked.

"Rick Patterson."

"You know this old man?"

"Sure. He's Deuce Taylor. We've been partners since last summer. We've been trapping in the mountains and we were headed for Casper. We just spent the night here. If you'll call off your dogs and get these guns out of our backs, we'll be sloping out of here."

"Yes, I expect you would like to," the pudgy man said. "Now tell me who's inside that cabin."

"Don't you tell him a thing, boy," Deuce yelled at me. "We don't know nuthin'."

"Shut up, Taylor." The pudgy man whirled to face him. "We're here on important business and we'll do what we have to do to get the information we want. It's all up to you and the kid. We've got the cabin surrounded, so it's only a question of time until we'll know anyhow."

Apparently the pudgy man was the leader of the bunch, a pompous bastard who figured he was important because he had the power on his side. More men had drifted up until I judged there were twenty-five or thirty around us. Anyway I looked at it, I couldn't see much sense in playing it tough.

"We might as well tell him what we know, Deuce," I said. "It's not much anyhow, and it won't make any difference to the others."

"That's right," the pudgy man said. "It might go a little easier on you if you cooperate."

"Cooperate with crawling scum like you?" Deuce said contemptuously. "I'd cooperate with a sidewinder sooner'n I would with you. Coming in here with an army of gunslingers to hang a bunch of innocent men and you want me to cooperate."

The pudgy man slapped him on the cheek, rocking his head. "Keep your mouth shut, old man." He turned back to me. "I'm Col. Walter Jessup," he said. "I'm in command of this expedition. Now you tell me what you know, or I'll turn some of my men loose on you."

"I'll tell you what I know," I said, "but like I just told you, it's not much. What I want to know is whether you're willing to dicker."

"No dicker," Jessup said. "Just talk."

"You don't want us," I said. "If I talk, will you turn us loose?"

I was scared, but I didn't want Jessup to know it. I was sure they were here to kill Coleman and Springer. Deuce and I would be witnesses, and that meant they wouldn't let us leave here alive. What I said or didn't say wouldn't make any difference. While I didn't really expect Jessup to release us, I aimed to pretend that I did.

"You've got a lot of gall, boy," Jessup said with a trace of admiration in his voice. "Now let me tell you how it is. You don't have any cards. They're all in our hands. We'd be crazy to talk about a dicker when we have nothing to gain and everything to lose. It was your hard luck to have spent this particular night here."

He waited a few seconds, then said impatiently, "You talking?"

"No," I said.

He turned and swung a hand toward a man who stood in the front row of the crowd. "Kid," he called, "come here." He wheeled back to me. "This is the Brazos Kid. He came up here from Texas to join our expedition. He's fought Apaches. He knows what to do with a man who won't talk. That right, Kid?"

"That's right," the Brazos Kid said as he drew a knife from its scabbard. "I've used this to cut a lot of calves, Colonel. Want I should make a gelding out of this scrub?"

The light was stronger now, strong enough for me to see the Brazos Kid clearly, too clearly. I'd never heard of him, which didn't mean anything either way, but I could believe all that Jessup had said about him. He had a narrow face with a very sharp chin and a sharp nose, but it was his eyes that scared me, tiny, black eyes that glittered with sheer pleasure when he talked about making a gelding out of me. I didn't doubt for a minute that he'd do it and enjoy every second of it.

Jessup didn't have time to answer. I said, "Put your knife away. All I know is that Matt Coleman and Bert Springer are inside."

"Just two of 'em?"

"That's all."

Jessup scratched his chin a moment as he considered this, then he said, "We could rush 'em and go on about our business."

"And get hell shot out of us," another man said.

Several others snickered. "You ought to know, Pete," one of them said.

I remembered Coleman saying some men had tried to kill him and he'd fought them off. The man called Pete must be Pete Martin who was accused of several killings in Smith County. Coleman had said that if he ever showed up here again, he'd be a dead man. Well, with this many hardcases backing him, I thought Coleman was mistaken.

The Brazos Kid still had his knife in his right hand. The forefinger of his left hand ran back and forth across the edge of the blade, gently caressing it as if it was something he loved very much. He said, "I dunno about this, Colonel. If you'd let me work on this sprout, he'd find plenty to talk about."

"No," Jessup said sharply. "He's said all I want to know. The problem is how to force them out of the cabin."

A man stationed around the corner of the barn said, "One of 'em's coming out now."

"Shoot him, Kid," Jessup said.

Several men including the Brazos Kid slid around the corner of the barn. The Kid slipped his knife back into the scabbard, drew his gun, and eased back the hammer. I was only a step or two behind him. I saw Springer walking toward the barn. He had gone about ten feet when suddenly he wheeled and bolted back toward the cabin. Something had tipped him off, I thought, and wondered what it was.

Springer made two long steps before the Brazos Kid fired. Springer lurched ahead one more step, then pitched forward on his face. Almost in that same instant Matt Coleman rushed outside, grabbed his partner by the shoulders, and hauled him into the cabin. A dozen guns opened up on him, but I didn't think he was hit.

"That's one of them," Jessup said with satisfaction. "Now we just have Coleman."

"We still ain't rushing that cabin," Martin said. "Coleman's as good as any ten men you'll ever find."

This time nobody snickered.

Jessup wheeled on me and motioned me back around the corner. He snapped, "A couple of you boys take these men inside the barn and tie them up." He turned away as if that disposed of both of us and bellowed an order, "Keep firing. We've got plenty of ammunition. Sooner or later a bullet is going to tag that rustling bastard."

"Come on, Ned," one of the men said as he stepped away from the others. "Help me put these two birds on ice till the Colonel wants 'em."

The two men pushed us through the back door of the barn, found some ropes, and tied our hands and feet. Our horses were in the stalls just as we had left them last night. Our rifles were still leaning against the wall in the corner, almost hidden from sight in the gloom of the interior of the barn. Apparently none of the invaders had seen them. We had left our hand guns in the cabin. Now, of course, there was no chance of recovering them.

The man who tied Deuce did a quick job and left, but the man tying me seemed to be all thumbs. He was the one who had told Ned to help him. I soon saw why he had volunteered so quickly. As soon as the other man left, this fellow said in a low tone, "I'm Hack Dunn. They sent somebody to Texas to recruit a gang of gunslingers and he came back with twenty-five men. They sent another one to Idaho and he came back with one. Me."

He rose, glanced at the door, and added, his voice still low, "I reckon you can get loose without much trouble. Watch your chance and ride out of here as soon as something happens that takes their attention off you."

"How come you're so damned anxious to get us out of the way?" Deuce demanded belligerently.

"Because my father was murdered by the same kind of high rollers these men are," Dunn said. "I hate 'em. I took a hand in this game figuring I might get back at 'em. Far as I'm concerned, they're all the same. Soon as it gets dark tonight, I'm pulling out for Grizzly to warn the sheriff."

He started toward the door, then paused and turned back. "You know you're dead men if you don't get out of here. Jessup had other things on his mind this morning, but after they get Coleman, he'll start thinking about you. He ain't gonna ride off and leave two men alive who can go to court and testify they saw Springer and Coleman murdered and can identify the murderers."

He went out, closing the back door of the barn. Deuce took a long breath. "By God, he's right. I'd rather get a slug in my guts riding out of here than to wait and have 'em shoot me cold turkey."

I was scared, more scared than I had ever been in my life. I'd been afraid plenty of times. I don't think any boy can grow up without being afraid of something, or many things as far as that goes. This was different. It had started when the Brazos Kid wanted to use his knife on me.

Now that I had time to think about it, I was more than just scared. The whole lower part of my belly felt as if it was frozen hard. I knew one thing for sure. Men who came here to murder in cold blood two cowboys who were accused of rustling would do anything. The chances were the Brazos Kid would have another chance to use his knife on me if I was still here.

This whole business was something I could not understand. I had taken Deuce's talk about an invasion with a dose of salt. The same with what Coleman and Springer had said last night. It just didn't seem possible that so-called civilized men would do this.

Wyoming was a state with all the governing functions that any state had. The old frontier days were gone, but Colonel Jessup and Pete Martin and the rest were all acting as if this was still the frontier with no law or law officers handling the rustling if there actually was any.

"Money and power," Deuce muttered. "They make a tough hand to beat just like Bert Springer said. Rick, you don't know these men, but I know a lot of 'em. The ones I don't know are the gunslicks from Texas like that son of the bitch of a Brazos Kid, but the rest of 'em are like Jessup. He owns the T-in-a-Box. They're ranch owners or foremen of big outfits in Smith and Natrona counties. Good men. Respectable men. The kind who hold all the political offices in Wyoming."

"I'm cold, Deuce," I said. "I feel like I want to puke, but my belly's all frozen up."

"You're cold because you're scared," Deuce said. "Roll over. I'll wiggle over to you and turn my back to you. I've got a little play in my fingers. I'll see if I can untie you."

I rolled over and began to twist my wrists back and forth. In a few seconds the rope fell away. Dunn hadn't really tied my wrists at all. I said, "I've done it, Deuce. I'll get the ropes off my ankles and then I'll untie you."

"I ain't one to think much about God," Deuce said, "but I guess it's time to thank Him for sending that Hack Dunn feller."

It took only a moment to untie my ankles, but the other man had done a good job of tying Deuce, so I pulled out my pocket knife and cut the ropes instead of taking time to struggle with the knots.

"We still ain't out of it by a hell of a lot," Deuce said. "I don't mind saying I'm scared, too, Rick. I've lived through some tight squeezes, but I always had a fighting chance. This time there's fifty men out there, and when we make a run for it, they'll all be shooting at us."

I walked to the wall nearest the cabin and, finding a knothole, put my right eye to it. The firing had not diminished. Men were all around the cabin just as Jessup had said, using any cover they could, boulders and the river bank and the thick brush that grew in several places along the river.

Coleman was answering the rifle fire, but he wasn't wasting any ammunition. Apparently he was trying to let them know he was still able to pull the trigger. He'd fire from one side of the cabin, then another, working his way around the inside of the big room.

Suddenly the fear in me began to fade. We had a chance, not much, but at least the fighting chance Deuce had talked about. I turned away from the knothole and said, "Deuce, let's get our horses saddled. I think we're going to have a chance to make a break pretty soon."

Deuce stared at me, wide-eyed. "Now what kind of a chance have we got riding through fifty men all trying to kill us. These men know how to shoot."

"You'll see," I said and, picking up my saddle, carried it to the sorrel.

As I tightened the cinch, I realized Deuce was right, but I had a funny feeling about this, funny because I knew anything was better than staying here. I would welcome a bullet. I hoped that bullet caught me dead center because I didn't want to live long enough to face the Brazos Kid's knife again.

11

THE MORNING dragged by. No one paid any attention to us, and that suited me fine. I worried about someone coming in and finding us free with our horse saddled, and then we'd be right back where we had been.

The interior of the barn was the wrong place to fight, but I decided I'd rather fight there than to be tied up again like a calf ready for branding, so I got the rifles and handed Deuce's to him.

"If anyone comes in, we'll make them work before they tie us up again," I said.

Deuce nodded. He was sitting on a pile of sacks of oats near the back door. I didn't know what was wrong with him, but the fight had gone out of him. He acted as if he was willing to take his medicine and like it.

I returned to my knothole, thinking that if Deuce wanted to roll over and play dead, he could, but I wasn't going to. The rifle fire had been almost continuous all morning, with Coleman shooting just enough to let them know he was alive and kicking. It seemed to me this was a standoff which could go on all day.

Coleman and Springer were two of the men the invaders wanted. I didn't doubt that, but it seemed to me that Jessup was showing poor judgment in letting two men hold the entire army of invaders here all day. A half dozen men could do as much as fifty could unless they rushed the cabin, and, from what Pete Martin had said, I was sure they had no intention of doing that.

The longer the invaders were held here, the less chance

there was that Grizzly would be surprised. Most of the men who were on the blacklist lived in town or in the surrounding area. At least that was what Coleman had said last night, and I figured he knew enough about it to make a smart guess. Springer was probably dead and Coleman would be in a matter of hours. It struck me that these two men were sacrificing their lives for the dozens of others on the list who lived farther north.

The more I hunkered there at the knothole and watched the puffs of smoke rising from the rifles of the invaders and listened to the steady cracking sound of the shots, the worse this whole murdering scheme seemed to me.

I was tempted to take a hand and knock off a few of the invaders I could see through the knothole, but I knew I'd gain nothing. I'd just put myself and Deuce into the same fix Coleman was in and not help him, either. If we had any chance at all, it lay in a surprise run, not in killing a few of the invaders which would only bring the anger of Jessup and his crew down on my head.

Sometime during the morning a cook wagon appeared from the Casper road that ran south along the river. It pulled in behind the barn, the cook jumped out and unhitched the team. A little later he started a fire and began fixing dinner.

Now the crazy freezing sensation in my belly was gone and I discovered I was hungry, but I sure wasn't going to ask for anything to eat. If we waited until dinner was cooked and most of Jessup's men gathered back of the barn to eat, somebody would bring us our meal and we'd be discovered.

I moved back and forth between my knothole in the wall facing the cabin and one I had found in the back wall facing the river. I decided we were going to have to make our break soon or it would be too late. Then, unexpectedly, our chance came, and in a manner I had not foreseen.

From somewhere to one side of the cabin the invaders had found a wagon which they had loaded with hay. They had fired the hay and now were pushing it toward the cabin. In a matter of minutes they'd have the cabin on fire and Coleman would either stay inside and be burned to death, or make a run for it and get shot to death.

"Come on, Deuce," I said. "This is the time we've been waiting for."

He kept sitting on the pile of oat sacks and blinking at me. I mounted and, leaning out of the saddle at the back door, used my knife to flip the turn pin. I pushed the door open and yelled, "Damn it, Deuce, are you going to sit there and let them shoot you full of holes?"

I never have understood what happened to Deuce, but he'd been acting as if he were in a daze. Now he came out of it and ran to his horse. "Go ahead," he said.

I bolted out of the barn, cracking steel to my sorrel for all I was worth. The cook was bending over the fire. I rode straight at him. He turned and yelled and scrambled to one side. I gave him a lick with my rifle barrel along the side of the head as I went past. He fell straight back toward the wagon and cracked his head on the hub as he went down.

A couple of men were walking toward the barn from the river. They were the only ones close enough to stop us and I decided I'd better play it as tough as I could. I guess they didn't know what was happening, or maybe they were too surprised to go for their guns. Anyhow, I rode straight at them just as I had at the cook, firing my rifle at every jump.

Not that I expected to hit either one because I knew from experience how hard it is to shoot straight from the back of a running horse, but I scared the bejabers out of them. They tried to run, fell down, and then scurried crablike toward the nearest boulder.

I didn't look back until I reached the brush and trees that bordered the bank. Several shots rattled through the leaves of the cottonwood above my head. I suppose some of the men had seen us and made a try at bringing us down, but it was poor shooting.

When I did glance back, I saw Coleman running away from the house. He had no place to go, but I guess he'd rather be shot to death than be burned up alive. I heard the increased volume of shots and saw Coleman stumble and fall, then we were into the brush and I couldn't see what happened after that.

We rammed through the fringe of brush to the water. It was shallow here as it was most of the time in Powder River. Deuce wasn't more than ten feet behind me now. We splashed across to the opposite bank, but we didn't have any trouble. I had counted on Coleman being the main attraction just at that time. I guess I was right; we made it to the east bank and turned south without any bullets coming close or anyone chasing us.

We slowed down after half a mile and pulled up to let our horses blow. We couldn't see anyone pursuing us, so we rode on at a slower pace, glancing back every minute or two, but no one appeared.

"Jessup had two choices," Deuce said. "He could send men after us and lose more time, or let us go and move on north. I guess that's what he decided to do."

"He's wasted too much time now if he's going to surprise Grizzy," I said. "I'll bet he never gets to Grizzy with his army."

"I ain't gonna take that bet," Deuce said. "I don't think he will, either. Now he's let two witnesses get away. I aim to testify, too. By God, I will. Matt Coleman was a good man and a friend of mine."

"You think they'll ever come to trial?" I asked.

He turned his head and stared at me thoughtfully, then he said, "You know, that's probably what Jessup's thinking. He could have sent a few men after us without holding the main army up, but he didn't figure it was worth it. You sure hit the nail on the head. He ain't figuring on being tried."

Still, we didn't know for sure what Jessup was thinking or what he'd do. He still might send someone after us, and if he did, his instructions would be to kill us. We pushed along as hard as we could all afternoon. We passed a number of ranches, but we didn't stop for a meal. It was better to keep moving and be hungry than to attract any attention.

That night we found a cave of sorts in a steep-walled gulch and built a small fire. Neither one of us felt like talking; we were tired and hungry and cold, and I think over all our discomforts was the nagging knowledge that Jessup and his friends were likely at some future time to decide we were too dangerous to be allowed to live.

We were fortunate that there was little wind, but the cold seemed to get worse before dawn and dig into the very marrow of our bones. No snow had fallen this far south, and that was lucky, too. I had a strange, haunting feeling as I huddled over the fire, that we had made a tragic mistake in stopping for the night at Coleman's and Springer's cabin, a mistake we would pay for as long as we lived.

Near daylight, I said, "Will we get to Casper tomorrow?"

"Sure," he answered, "if we don't have any more hard luck."

"We're about broke," I said. "We've lost our furs and pack animals."

Deuce swore. "No way to get 'em back, neither." He wiped a hand across his mouth and said, "I knew better'n to stop there last night. I had a dream before we started out, a dream about me being chased and getting caught and being strung up. We should have kept on going."

That was crazy reasoning, I thought. It was plain hindsight. He'd had no way of knowing what lay ahead, of what the dream was telling him if it was telling him anything at all, but now I knew why he had quit back there in the barn and gone into that daze, acting like there was no hope and he was just waiting for them to come and kill us.

We started south again before sunup and kept at it all day, stopping now and then to blow the horses. I wasn't hungry, not the way I had been, but I kept thinking that Coleman and Springer had been murdered, we had seen the killing, and we knew who did it. They wouldn't let us ride off in peace, not after what we had seen and could testify to.

It was probably true that Jessup thought none of them would be brought to trial, but how could he avoid it? Why did he think that? Well, one way was to see to it that there were no witnesses.

I remembered the man and woman who had been lynched over on the Sweetwater. None of the lynchers had been tried. Why? Because all of the witnesses had disappeared or died in some mysterious manner soon after the lynching.

No answer came to me that made me feel any better. The invaders would see to it that no one was alive who was able to testify against them. The familiar frozen feeling came back into my belly. I guess that was why I wasn't hungry.

Once when we stopped, I said, "Deuce, I've been thinking, but it sure isn't a pleasant thought. They're going to start chasing us and they'll keep at it until they find us and kill us."

"So that's what you've had buzzing around in your head," Deuce said. "I keep thinking about my dream. I guess that's what it was saying to me."

"We'd better not stay in Wyoming," I said. "We'd better head for Colorado."

Deuce snorted in derision. "On tired horses? With us broke and having nothing to eat for two days?"

"Well, what are we going to do?" I demanded. "I've got seven dollars and some change in my pocket. We can't find much of a place to hole up for that."

"I've got five dollars and some change," he said. "That would get me a smaller hole than your seven dollars will buy."

"If we stop in Casper and go to work, providing we did find jobs, they'd run us down without any trouble and they'd kill us."

"One thing's sure," he said. "We've got to hole up somewhere." He was silent a moment, looking out across the sagebrush, then he added slowly, "I know a woman in Casper who owes me a favor. I think she'll give us a place to stay for a few days. By that time we'll know how the mob made out when it got to Grizzly. Our horses will be rested and we can go on if it seems to be the thing to do."

"I hope she can cook good," I said. "I'm going to be

hungry when I'm warm and I know I'm safe. Right now I'm cold, but I'm not sure whether it's from the weather or because I'm scared."

"We've got plenty of reason for being scared," Deuce said. "One other thing worries me. You're kind o' young to be going with me. This woman's a madam. She runs a whorehouse and I ain't sure she'll let you in."

"I'm twenty-one," I said. "She won't know I'm lying. I look it, don't I?"

"Yeah, you look it, all right," Deuce said, "but I ain't sure I've got any business taking you to a whorehouse."

"It's better'n getting murdered," I said.

He nodded and quit arguing. I spent some time thinking about how it would be, living in a whorehouse, and decided it would be mighty interesting. The truth was I really didn't give much thought to any business I might give the girls. I was just too cold and miserable. All I could think of was a warm fire, a good meal, and a decent bed.

A little while after dark we topped a ridge and looked down at the lights of Casper. It was just about the most beautiful sight I ever saw in my whole life.

12

We KEPT OFF the streets as much as possible, using the alleys so that we came to the back of the house Deuce had mentioned. He said, "The madam's name is Ellie. She's no spring chicken anymore. I think she quit working several years ago when she got so fat she had trouble going through a door, but she's honest, which same is more'n I can say for some madams I've known."

I couldn't see his face in the darkness, but I heard him snicker. He went on, "She calls her house the Pleasure Palace. I guess it's a purty good name 'cause they sure furnish pleasure, but the house ain't no palace."

I heard him dismount. He opened the barn door and a moment later a match flared. He grunted in satisfaction, then he said, "I always used to keep a lantern on this nail when I worked for Ellie, and, by God, it's still there."

He jacked up the chimney, touched the flame to the wick, and then lowered the chimney. "Come on," he said. "There's plenty of space for our horses. She used to have a bay gelding she had for buggy riding. He's still here, too."

He snickered again, and added, "She never worries about nothing. Let the women of town talk all they want to. She used to have me harness up her horse and hook him to the buggy, then she'd go sashaying down Main Street, wearing a big hat with a long plume. She never spoke to her customers when she seen 'em on the street, though she'd always speak to the Methodist preacher and smile like she knew him real well."

I got down, though it was an effort. I was that stiff from

the cold. I asked, "Did it ever occur to you that she might not like us moving in on her?"

"Naw," he scoffed. "She'll be glad to see us."

We put our horses away, watering them from a trough at the end of the runway. We filled their mangers with hay, Deuce blew out the lantern, and we left the barn, closing the door behind us.

We crossed the backyard to the door, and it struck me that I still didn't know what kind of favor Deuce had done for this woman that she would give him a place to hole up. If he didn't volunteer the information, I was damned if I was going to ask.

Deuce knocked on the back door. A tall, middle-aged woman opened it and stared at Deuce. She said, "If you're here on business, go around to the front door." He still stood there, waiting, the lamplight falling across his face, and then the woman let out a howl you could have heard a block away.

"Deuce," she shouted. "Deuce Taylor, you old reprobate, get in here so I can shut the door and keep the cold out."

He went in. I was a step behind him. The woman shut the door and hugged Deuce, then he introduced me and the woman shook my hand. Her name was Maude, and from the conversation I judged she had been a housekeeper for the Pleasure Palace for a long time.

"Well Deuce, you old fraud, you look cold," Maude said. "Get over here by the fire. Pull up a chair. Ellie will be glad to see you."

"I hope so," he said. "We've been doing a lot of riding and we ain't et in two days. We need a place to stay where nobody'll look for us."

"So you're in trouble with the law," Maude said. "I declare, Deuce, you're old enough to stay out of trouble. You must be past ninety, ain't you?"

Deuce snorted and held his hands out over the fire. He winked at me. "You see?" he said. "They like me here. No woman is gonna insult a man by saying he's ninety when he comes to her whorehouse if she didn't like him."

Maude was trotting back and forth between the pantry

and the kitchen, putting food on the table. She said, "Well now, I dunno about that. It's them that's ninety who are the best around here. They've got to be because they take so much time, but I ain't sure that makes anybody like 'em." She glanced at me, laughing. "From the time Deuce used to take, he must be more'n ninety."

I didn't say anything. I didn't laugh as I was supposed to, either. My face felt as if it was frozen stiff and now that it was thawing, I just didn't feel like responding to Maude's humor. I looked at the roast she'd brought out, the crock of milk, the loaf of bread and plate of butter, the dish of jam and the custard pie, and it was all I could do to keep from going to the table and start shoveling it in.

"Well, there it is," Maude said. "It's cold, but it'll have to do. I'll make a pot of coffee. Ellie always wants some after the crowd leaves."

From the front of the house I heard a piano being played and a girl singing some old, sentimental songs. As we sat down and started to eat, Maude said, "They're just getting warmed up now. It'll be three, four hours before they all finish and Ellie gets free to come in here and have her coffee."

"How's business?" Deuce asked.

"Booming," Maude answered. "She gets some of the best businessmen in Casper. She's got some new girls, three of 'em who came in from Cheyenne about a year ago, and a brand new little filly named Lisa." She looked at me, speculatively, I thought, as if wondering just how good a man I was, and added, "You'll cotton to her, sonny. She's just about your age. Trouble is a girl like her don't ever stay in a place like this."

We ate like two pigs, and after while I realized I'd have a bellyache if I kept on, so I sat back and filled my pipe. I said, "Deuce, you'd better stop for breath or you'll founder yourself."

He heaved a sigh and wiped the back of his hand across his mouth as he stared longingly at what was left of the custard pie. "Yeah, I guess you're right. Maude, I never ate a better meal in my life. Did you ever go two days without eating?"

"No," she answered, "and I don't figger on doing it, either. I enjoy my victuals."

"So do I," Deuce said, "when I can get 'em."

I pulled on my pipe and smelled the coffee boiling on the stove and the next thing I knew my head was tipping forward and my pipe fell out of my hand. I woke with a start and heard Maude laugh.

"Mebbe you ain't slept any more'n you et," Maude said.

"I didn't last night," I admitted.

"We're lucky to be alive," Deuce said. "I reckon we'll take that coffee later. If you can show us which room to take, we'll roll in."

Maude scratched her head and frowned. "All the beds upstairs are being used," she said. "Guess I'll have to put you down in the cellar. Ain't no bed there, but you can make out on an old mattress. I can give you plenty of quilts."

"We ain't choosey," Deuce said.

"Come on," Maude said as she picked up the lamp and opened a door at the other end of the kitchen.

We followed her down a flight of rickety stairs into a cellar that had a dirt floor and dirt walls and felt cold and musty, but, as Deuce said, we weren't choosey. Maude set the lamp on a shelf and began pulling quilts out of a drawer in a massive bureau.

"These are all extras," she said. "We used some of 'em in the winter and thought spring was here, but I guess it ain't made it yet. If you're gonna be sponging off Ellie, I'll put you to work in her garden tomorrow."

"It's too early," Deuce said. "Like you said, spring ain't made it yet."

"It ain't too early to spade the garden," Maude said crisply, "and haul horse manure and you know it. We ain't had a man around here lately, and I ain't gonna do that kind of work. I've got more'n I can do keeping the house up and feeding strays that wander in after nine o'clock."

"We're obliged, ma'am," I said. "We'll be glad to do any work you set us to."

"Well now, Deuce," Maude said, "that's the kind of attitude I like to hear, and I never did hear it from you. I'll wake you bright and early in the morning."

"Not in the morning," Deuce said, "on account of we're gonna sleep. Any other morning we'll roll out and go to work, but not tomorrow."

I sat down on the makeshift bed and pulled off my boots. I crawled in between the blankets, so groggy I didn't make any sense out of what Deuce and Maude were saying to each other. That was all I knew for about twelve hours. When I woke, a woman was holding a lantern at the foot of the stairs looking down at us.

"Wake up, lazy bones," she boomed. "I know you told Maude you wanted to sleep this morning, but this is ridiculous."

Deuce opened one eye, yelled, "Ellie," and threw back the covers. He jumped up and hugged her, and she hugged him and kissed him and cried a little, and I decided he hadn't been fooling me when he said Ellie liked him.

She was the fattest woman I ever saw, oozing flesh any place I looked. She had monstrous bosoms that she didn't worry about keeping covered. It looked to me as if she wasn't wearing anything except a heavy wool robe, and it was open about halfway down the front, so I had an impression she had swallowed Deuce between those immense breasts.

I got up and Deuce introduced us. Ellie looked me over and said, "If you're a friend of this ornery, no good old cuss, you're welcome to stay here as long as you want to. I don't mind saying right now that we've got some work around here that needs doing. I guess I knew you were coming. I ain't hired a man all winter."

"We'll work," I said. "We're that glad to have a place to hole up."

"Maude told me you was in some kind of trouble," Ellie said. "Come on up to the kitchen and have a cup of coffee and tell me about it."

We grabbed our boots and followed her up the stairs. Maude was pouring coffee for three women who were sprawled around the kitchen table. All of them were wearing robes and hadn't bothered to fix their hair. They weren't any more modest than Ellie. Cows! That's what they were. About thirty. Ugly. Big-boned. I didn't know much about whores, but most of the ones I'd seen looked about the same as these.

Then a door opened and a girl came in. Right away I knew it was a mistake to generalize about whores. This one was close to my age. She was slim and pretty and wore a white-and-pink gingham dress that any housewife might have worn. Her blond hair was brushed and tied behind her head. The instant our eyes met, I think we had the same thought. We were going to be friends.

Ellie introduced us to all the women. The cows grunted something. One of them belched as she raised the coffee cup to her mouth. The girl, Lisa, smiled and shook hands with us, letting her hand linger in mine a little longer than necessary. I guess I had the question any man would have when he looked at her. How did she happen to land up in this place?

Deuce and I sat down at the table and Maude poured coffee for us and set a plate of doughnuts in front of us. The three cows got up and left, but Lisa sat down across the table from me and drank a cup of coffee.

"Now then," Ellie said, "I'm going to hear what kind of a fix you're into, but you'd better know right now that I have never harbored a man running from the law. I don't figure on getting into trouble with the law now if you're a wanted man."

Deuce told the whole story, starting clear back in Miles City, and wound up by saying, "I figure we're wanted men, all right, but not by the law."

Ellie wiped her eyes. "I'll tell you right now that you can stay here just as long as you want to. Getting into trouble with the Association may be worse than getting into trouble with the law, but I don't give a damn. Matt Coleman and Bert Springer were friends of mine, God rest their souls."

She wiped her eyes again, and added, "You know, the train that hauled them bastards up here from Cheyenne was supposed to be a big secret, but there was some rumors running around about the kind of business you got into, so I reckon they was all true, though I didn't believe 'em when I heard 'em. It just didn't seem that the kind of men who run this state and belong to the Association would set out to commit cold-blooded murder."

"They done it, though," Deuce said.

I drank three cups of coffee and ate six doughnuts, and said, "Now about this work you want done."

We spent the next three days doing all kinds of odd jobs from moving the privy and fixing the cellar stairs down to spading the garden and cleaning out the stable and hauling horse manure to the garden in a wheelbarrow.

Ellie staked out enough work to keep us going all spring, I guess. I enjoyed myself. The weather turned warm, Maude was a good cook, and although I despised the three cows, Lisa was a joy to be with. I guess she liked me because she hung around me when I was working. I worked, too. Fact is, I did most of it. Deuce was a genius when it came to finding excuses for not working.

Then we heard what had happened to the invaders. The wires had been cut, but they were finally repaired and the whole story came in. The invaders had burned the Circle A buildings and gone on north to the T-in-a-Box. Several men had ridden past the Circle A when the shooting was going on and had reached Grizzly with the story. B.U. Joyful had passed out rifles and ammunition to the men who needed either, and about two hundred townsmen and small ranchers surrounded the invaders who had holed up in the T-in-a-Box buildings. They'd have been massacred if the soldiers hadn't arrived from Fort McKinney and rescued them.

"They oughtta be strung up," Ellie muttered. "The whole passel of them."

"I heard they'll be tried for murder," Lisa said, "and they need all the witnesses they can find."

I looked at Deuce and Deuce looked at me. I guess the

same thought that was in my mind was in Deuce's. Sure, if we lived we could testify and help put a rope around the neck of every one of Col. Jessup's men, but the chances were we wouldn't live that long. We didn't say anything. Another three days went by, Deuce getting boogery and not talking and sitting off by himself while I was working.

One evening he didn't go to bed when I did. He sat in the kitchen, staring at the wall and acting as if he didn't see a thing. I got up and said I was going to bed.

"I ain't ready yet, Rick," he said. "You go ahead."

"You'll go floating down the stairs with all that coffee you've been drinking," Maude said.

"I'll change it to whiskey if you've got any," Deuce said.

"We don't," Maude said. "Not for nobody but cash customers."

"I ain't that," Deuce said. Then he looked at me. "Rick, we've got to ride up there to Grizzly and tell 'em what we seen. I reckon we're the best witnesses they've got."

"We're not doing any such thing," I said. "It would be committing suicide and you know it. Ellie says we can stay here and keep under cover and that's what I'm going to do."

"I figgered we'd go to the marshal here and tell him," Deuce said. "Or the sheriff. They could arrange to give us an escort to Grizzly."

"Sure they would," I said, "but we'd never get there. I know how you feel, but if we're going to live long enough to tell our story, we'd better wait till we know if anybody's listening."

"Yeah, reckon you're right," he said, but from his tone of voice I knew I had not convinced him.

I went to bed, thinking he could do exactly as he pleased. He was an old man. Maybe he was ready to die, but I wasn't. Still, I lay awake a long time thinking about it and getting a little uneasy. I thought I knew Deuce pretty well. We'd been together for about nine months. It was the kind of relationship in which we couldn't keep much about ourselves from the other one. I just didn't think he'd do what he did.

It was after midnight when I woke up. Lisa was holding a lamp and bending over me. She said, "Rick, Deuce is gone."

I sat up. "Where?"

"I'd like to get in bed with you," she said. "I'll tell you about it."

I threw back the top quilts and moved over. "Come ahead," I said.

She blew out the lamp and lay down beside me. She shivered and whispered, "I'm cold."

I reached over and touched her. She didn't have anything on. I slipped my arm around her and pulled her to me. "I'll get you warm," I said. "Now tell me about it."

"Ellie says he's gone to the sheriff to tell him what he saw when Coleman and Springer were killed," Lisa said.

"Then they'll be coming after me, too," I said. "I'd better pull out."

"No, he told Ellie that you were free to do what you want to," Lisa said. "He said he wasn't going to say a word about you. You stay right here. You're the first decent thing that's happened since I've been here."

Then she started kissing me and I didn't have any time to think about Duece. Maybe I wouldn't have anyhow. He was a stubborn old coot. I'd found out more than once that I couldn't change him once he made up his mind about something and I sure didn't aim to try now.

While I was eating breakfast the following morning, Ellie brought me a .45 and a gun belt with every loop filled with a cartridge. She said, "A man left this here one time when he didn't have any money to pay his bill. He'd been coming here on tick for quite a while so he had a hell of a bill. I didn't want his gun, but it was that or turn him over to the marshal and I didn't want to do that, so I took the gun. You'd better take it, Rick. I don't want one of them murdering bastards coming after you and you not having anything to defend yourself with."

"I don't have any money . . . ," I began.

She waved me into silence. "Pay me when you can. I

just don't want you to be a sitting duck for 'em if they come after you."

I thanked her and buckled the gun belt around me. It was the first time I'd felt fully dressed since Deuce and I had got away from the mob in Smith County.

13

THE NEXT DAY I asked Ellie what Deuce had said before he lit out. She shook her head. "I can't tell you. I mean, I don't remember the exact words he used, but it was something about never having been at a place where important things happened. What happened at the Circle A was important. Matt Coleman and Bert Springer had been good friends of his, and he aimed to see somebody hung for their murder."

"So he went to the sheriff?"

She nodded. "I told him the sheriff would do anything the Association wanted him to, but he didn't believe me. In this state you'll never hang a man like Col. Jessup. I don't care how many murders he commits."

She cocked her head and stared at me thoughtfully, then she said, "Rick, you're safe as long as they don't know you're here, but if they make Deuce tell 'em about you, or if they happen to spot you, you're in trouble."

"Then I'd better start moving," I said.

"Not yet. You're a good worker and I like to have you here." She kind of grinned and added, "Lisa likes you. I'm afraid she's not going to stay much longer. Maybe your being here will help keep her here. I'll take care of you if it comes to a showdown."

I figured she would, too, if she could. Anyhow, I stayed because I hoped we'd hear something about Deuce. The showdown was bound to come sooner or later, and as the next week passed I got a little more uneasy all the time because I had a hunch that the longer I stayed, the more of a chance I was taking.

Every morning sometime between midnight and sunup Lisa got into bed with me. I'd never had anything like it and I tell you I thought it was great, but it wasn't heaven by a long shot because I couldn't forget that the Association would put a killer on my tail and sooner or later he'd find out where I was hiding. The only way I could stay alive was to get out of the state.

I told Lisa that one night about a week after Deuce left. She said, "Take me out of here, Rick. I can't go on living this way."

"I can't take you anywhere," I said. "I've got seven dollars in my pocket. How long could we live on that?"

"I'll get some money," she promised. "We can take Ellie's horse. There's a saddle in the barn. He can be ridden. I've done it. I'm a good rider. You don't have to marry me or anything. Just get me out of here."

I thought about that for a while. Ellie would be sore at me if I took Lisa. She'd be more than sore if I stole her horse. It would be stupid to take Lisa. I could always make some kind of living for myself, but a living for me and a woman was something else. So I told myself I wasn't going to do it, and then I knew right away I was going to try.

It wasn't logical and I'd probably be on the run the rest of my life unless I had a chance to testify and be protected, but I didn't think that was possible. Still I liked Lisa and had from the first minute I'd seen her. Having her in bed with me every night, well, I couldn't beat that.

"All right," I said. "When do you want to go?"

"Tomorrow night," she said. "As soon as everybody's asleep. I'll get a sack of grub and we'll slip out the back. They won't know we're gone until the next morning."

She gripped my arms and whispered, "Ellie didn't tell you, but she went to the sheriff's office and asked about Deuce. They pretended they'd never heard of him. She saw a strange man there, a young fellow, sharp nose, sharp chin, a real tough, she said. They were calling him the Brazos Kid. You don't see many men like that around

Casper, so she wondered if he was an Association man.
Did you ever hear of him?"

My heart dropped clear out of sight when she said that.
Col. Jessup and the rest figured I was around here somewhere, and they must have sent the Brazos Kid after me
before they were surrounded by the army at the T-in-a-
Box. I knew I should have pulled my freight a week ago
when Deuce left, but that was a good case of hindsight.

"Yeah, I've heard of him," I said. "Let's get out of here
now. Ellie's dead right about him. He was at the Circle A
with the mob when they killed Coleman and Springer."

"No, we won't leave now," she said. "Tomorrow
night."

"Why not right now?" I wanted to know.

She put her finger tips over my mouth. "I'm not ready
yet. That's why. I will be tomorrow night. Don't tell Ellie
or Maude or anybody. We'll just slip out and we'll be
miles away when they find out we're gone."

I let it go at that, but I had a feeling it was a mistake to
wait. It was, too, damned near a fatal mistake. I worked
in the house the same as usual the next day, painting the
hall and the stairs that led to the girls' rooms. I hadn't
been outside much since Deuce left, figuring somebody
might be watching the house. I waited until dark to do
anything that had to be done outside such as taking care
of the horses.

By the time I finished supper it was beginning to turn
dusk, I sat at the table with Maude drinking coffee. Ellie
and the girls had gone upstairs to get prettied up for the
night's business. I heard the door bell. Maude didn't, or
pretended she didn't. She was in the middle of a long story
about the early days in Cheyenne when she'd been a
housekeeper for the finest whorehouse in town. I guess she
didn't want to stop.

"Better get the door," I said.

"Oh hell." She got up and glanced at the clock on the
wall. "It's too early for anyone to come on business. I
don't know why anybody would be ringing that bell
now."

She left the kitchen. I got up and took my gun belt off a

nail by the door. I don't know why I did it except that what Maude said made me uneasy. A moment later I heard her yell that it was too early for anybody to come for business, then a man yelled back that he wasn't here for house business. He was here on official business and she'd better get out of the way.

I guess she didn't. He must have hit her. Her scream sounded as if he'd hurt her, then she yelled, "Rick! Come here and help me."

I'd finished buckling my gun belt and had drawn my gun when the hall door slammed open. A man lunged through it into the kitchen, stumbling a little as if he was off balance. I guess the door came open easier than he had expected. He was wearing a star and had a gun in his hand. The first thought that raced through my mind was that he hadn't come here to arrest me. He was here to kill me.

I didn't waste time asking questions. I let him have it through the belly. I shot him again as he fell. He fired, the bullet plowing into the floor. Maude ran into the kitchen, stopped, looked at him, and then at me. I knelt beside him, still holding my gun. Blood ran out of his mouth and down his chin.

He tried to say something. I wasn't sure what it was, but I thought he said they'd get me. Maude came out of it then and yelled at me, "You idiot! That's Vance Boyle. He's the deputy sheriff. They'll hang you for this."

I forgot all about Lisa. I just knew I had to make tracks and make them in a hurry. I holstered my gun and grabbed my hat off a nail by the back door as Ellie and the girls, all half dressed or less, ran into the kitchen. I didn't want to say good-bye. I yanked my sheepskin off the wall and raced out through the back door and across the porch.

By the time I hit the ground, I knew my hunch about the deputy was right because the Brazos Kid was standing by the barn door. The light was thin, but I couldn't mistake that hatchet face of his. He didn't stop to explain anything to me, either. He started shooting.

The bastard had me dead to rights if he'd taken more

time or waited till I got closer, but he was impatient and started firing the instant I was off the porch. He had two clean shots before I could get my gun out of leather and he missed them both. I didn't miss. I don't know where I hit him, but he went back and down, his gun dropping out of his hand as he fell.

I thought he was dead when I ran by him. I didn't stop to look close because he wasn't moving. I dropped my gun into the holster and picked up his gun and shoved it under my waistband. I ran into the barn and saddled my sorrel as fast as I could, figuring there might be more of them around. Even if there wasn't, Ellie would notify the sheriff and he'd be here in a hurry.

When I backed my sorrel out of the stall, I saw Lisa standing in the doorway. She cried, "You're not going to leave me?"

I didn't have time to argue or explain anything. The truth was I had completely forgotten her. I let the reins dangle and threw Ellie's saddle on the bay. As I tightened the cinch, I knew what I was doing. If they caught us, we'd get it for horse stealing.

I'd seen enough of Ellie to know that along with that easygoing way of hers there was a vindictive streak in her a yard wide. If I'd have had time to think about it, I probably would have told Lisa I couldn't take her, but I didn't have time. Besides, I had a feeling that it would be rough on her if I didn't take her.

Anyhow, we were out of there in a matter of seconds. I don't know if Ellie saw us or not, but I don't think she did. She'd have started shooting if she had. Besides, she was probably trying to figure out what to do with a dead deputy in the kitchen and what the sheriff would do when he got there.

"I want to get across the Colorado line as fast as we can," I said. "Do you know the road?"

"Yes," she said, and took the lead. "We'll follow the river."

The moon was almost full, so we kept a good pace through most of the night. Lisa could ride. I'd just had her word for it, but she hadn't lied to me. She knew the country, too. When the sun was beginning to show, she said, "We'd better hole up. Let's get over yonder to the river."

We found a small meadow along the river with a fringe of willows that would keep us from being seen by anyone riding on the road. I stepped down and gave Lisa a hand. She took a few steps and groaned.

"It's been a while since I was on a horse," she said. "I'm softer than I thought I was."

She lifted her skirt and rubbed the inside of her thighs, then she collapsed on the ground. She looked up at me, grimacing, and said, "I'm sorry, Rick. I just got to the end of the line."

I stripped gear from the horses, watered them, and staked them out, then I went to Lisa who was sprawled on the ground. We were in the same fix Deuce and I had been in when we left the Circle A. We were on the run and we didn't have anything to eat. The only difference was that the weather had turned warm and that was something to be thankful for.

"We're in trouble," I said. "Ellie's not going to favor the idea of us stealing her horse. We may be the second man-woman team to be strung up in Wyoming."

"Trouble's not new to me," she said. "Or you, either, I guess." She reached inside her blouse and drew out a buckskin bag. She tapped it against her hand, laughing softly. "How do you like the sound of gold coins hitting gold coins? Nice, isn't it?"

"Where'n hell did you get 'em?" I demanded. "If you did what I think you did . . ."

"That's exactly what I did," she said. "I got into Ellie's bureau drawer as soon as I heard the first shot and she ran out of her room. I knew where she kept her money. She never lets very much accumulate, so there's probably not more than a hundred dollars, but it'll help."

"So we're worse than horse thieves," I said. "We steal money, too."

"You're damn right," she said, "and I wish there had been more to steal. Do you know that Ellie never paid me

off, saying she'd settle up later, so I think I'm still behind,
but it was the best I could do."

I sat down on the grass beside Lisa. I didn't know what
to say. I did know that Ellie wouldn't see it the way Lisa
did. I figured I'd done enough work for Ellie to justify
taking her old bay, but she wouldn't see that, either. We
had quite a bit against us, enough to keep us running. A
murder charge along with horse stealing and taking Ellie's
gold.

"What do you want to do?" I asked. "We've got to stay
here all day and it's a long ways to the Colorado line."

"I want to do the only thing we can," she said. "We'll
hole up during the day and we'll ride at night, and sooner
or later we're going to get to Colorado."

"We'll get hungry," I said.

"I've been hungry," she said. "There's worse things
than being hungry. You can shoot some rabbits or sage
hens or anything else you can find to keep us eating. We'll
make it. Just one thing I've got to know, Rick. Are you
going to keep me or turn me loose in the first town we
come to?"

"I've got you," I said. "I guess I might as well keep
you."

"Good," she said. "It's the only thing I've been worried
about. I couldn't stand another night living the way I had
been. You don't know what it's like to go to bed with
drunks and men who haven't bathed for weeks." She
closed her eyes. Tears ran down her cheeks. "I've
dreamed about finding a man like you, but I didn't think I
ever would."

I guess a lot of folks could never understand this, me
being thankful to have a girl like Lisa, her being what she
was, but I was thankful. I never regretted taking her,
either.

14

WE MADE IT to Colorado by the grace of God or sheer good luck or maybe because we were careful. Perhaps it was a combination of all three. We followed the North Platte as much as we could, we stopped at a ranch and traded Ellie's old bay for another horse, a gray about as old and worn out as the bay, and we bought supplies from a small country store.

We followed the river because it gave us a place to hide during the day. If we'd cut directly across the sagebrush hills, we could have been seen for miles. We traded horses because I didn't want to be caught with a stolen horse in our possession, so any kind of a trade was an advantage to us. We paid the rancher twenty dollars. I didn't like to cut down our small amount of money, but we had to sweeten the pot to make the trade. We bought supplies because a diet of jack rabbit meat was mighty monotonous.

We sat up and talked instead of sleeping the first day we camped in Colorado. We were tired of being careful, tired of riding at night and hiding out all day, tired of continually looking back over our shoulders to see if we were being followed. Not that we were absolutely safe, but at least a Wyoming sheriff wouldn't be after us once we were across the state line.

We knew we could be tracked, but we had the advantage of picking the direction of our flight. Anybody tracking us had to pick up the trail first by guessing which way we went, and the most likely guess was that we had ridden east to Douglas. Even after they learned we had gone south, they had to make another guess after we reached the railroad. We could have gone into Laramie and taken the train either east or west and we'd have been hundreds of miles away by now.

Maybe we were whistling in the dark. The only thing I knew for sure was that I had been marked for death and sooner or later the killer would pick up my trail. Traveling with a woman was bound to make it easier to track me, but I didn't tell Lisa that.

For the time being we felt safe, so we built a fire in the daytime and cooked a meal. After that we lay under the tall cottonwoods and listened to the wind in the branches and the faint rustle of water as the North Platte flowed by.

We talked. Just getting acquainted, I guess. I told Lisa about my childhood and how I'd run away from home after my mother died and that I still didn't know whether I had killed my stepfather or not. When I said that, she sat up and stared at me, her eyes wide.

She said, "Rick, this is impossible. Listening to you is like hearing about my life." She swallowed and, picking up a stick, began to jab at the soft earth. Then she said, "I've been asked hundreds of times, I guess, how I happened to work in a whorehouse. Men liked to say that a pretty girl like me could get married and have a home, as if getting married was certain to be a good thing.

"I could have been married dozens of times. I had ten proposals in the short time I worked for Ellie, but there wasn't one of them that promised anything but hard work and poverty and misery. Men like that are glad to marry a fallen woman and pretend they're doing her a favor by giving her their name. Of course they'd throw it up to her the rest of her life. Hell, all they really want is a housekeeper and a woman to sleep with who don't cost them anything. The right man who could give a woman a decent home wouldn't look at me if he saw me on the street."

Her face turned sad and I thought she was going to cry. She didn't. Not then. She said in a low, bitter voice, "I've been an outcast since I was fifteen. My mother died and an uncle took me into his home. His wife was an invalid.

One time I was in the barn hunting for eggs when he came in and grabbed me.

"I screamed and fought and bit him, but I couldn't get free until he was done with me. I told him I was going to kill him. He laughed at me and said his wife wasn't any use to him, but I was. I picked up a pitchfork and ran it into his belly. I think I killed him. I didn't stay to find out. I ran into the house and got my things and left."

She stopped and looked at the water that was running deep and swift right there. She was silent a long time, thinking about it, I guess. Finally she went on, "I appreciate your not asking me why I was in Ellie's place. You see, it was that or kill myself. What can a fifteen-year-old girl do to earn her living?

"After I'd been raped I didn't think any man would want me. When I got so tired of being hungry and cold that I couldn't stand it any longer, I went to a madam in Cheyenne and told her I was eighteen. She put me to work. After I'd been there almost three years, I thought Casper might be better, but it wasn't because Ellie is a tough old bitch. I'd been thinking of stealing her horse and all the money I could and leave, but I was afraid to go alone, so I waited and you came along."

I figured she'd been wanting to tell me all this before, but she'd been afraid to. After she had told it, I think she was relieved. She started to cry after she got it said. I took her into my arms and kissed her and held her hard against me. She went to sleep that way, and I thought that what she had been didn't make any difference to me. She was my woman now.

Later that day I asked her one other question that I'd been curious about. I had wanted to ask Deuce, but I'd never worked up enough nerve, thinking that he'd get around to telling me in his own good time. He never had.

"What kind of favor had Deuce done for Ellie that he was so sure she'd hide him?" I said.

"It's an unlikely story," she said, "because Deuce was pretty much of a fraud as you've probably figured out. He'd worked for Ellie about a year. She didn't give him much more than his board and room, and, the way Maude tells it, that was more than he was worth. Ellie was always jawing at him for one thing or another, and finally she got enough of it and fired him. He took it pretty hard, not having much money and not knowing what to do or where to go, but he finally packed up the few things he had and went out and saddled his horse.

"I guess he took a long time, not wanting to go and thinking maybe Ellie would change her mind, but nothing happened. Finally he was just about ready to get on his horse and leave when he heard some horrible screaming from the house. He ran into the parlor and found a man who was stark naked brandishing a knife. He'd cut one girl pretty bad and he had Ellie backed into a corner telling her he was going to cut her heart out.

"Deuce shot him. It was the most worthwhile thing he'd done for Ellie and she promised him that if he ever needed a place to stay, she'd put him up. She even offered his old job back, but he got contrary and said he guessed he'd ride up into Smith County. That's the last she saw of him till he rode in with you."

"Does Ellie have any idea what's happened to him?"

"It's just a guess, but she thinks the deputy that you killed took him north promising to protect him until he reached Smith County. She thinks the deputy shot and killed him and buried him out there where nobody will ever find his body."

I nodded. I'd come to the same conclusion. I hoped the man I'd shot was the man who had done it. It seemed a fitting kind of justice if it had been that way. Again it was guessing, but I had a hunch that the deputy and the Brazos Kid came to Ellie's house because she had gone to sheriff's office and asked about Deuce.

It was a matter of putting two and two together. She knew Deuce had gone to the sheriff, so when she showed up asking about him, they figured he had been staying with Ellie. The next guess was that I had been with Deuce, so I must be there, too.

The deputy had been stupid, going at it the way he had. He could have arrested me on some trumped-up charge and killed me later, but there are plenty of stupid men wearing stars. Maybe the Brazos Kid had talked him into coming after me the way he had. That would have been his way of doing it.

We stayed there all of that day and that night because it was a pleasant, restful place. We relaxed for the first time since we'd left Casper. The next day we rode south into North Park. I started asking for work, but it was several days later before I got a job in a sawmill in the south edge of the park. I didn't like the work, but they gave us a log cabin to live in, and there was a store handy, so we decided it was a pretty good deal even though it was too close to Wyoming.

Lisa told me she wasn't a very good cook or house-keeper, but she soon learned. Maybe this wasn't heaven, either, because I put in long, hard hours in that damned sawmill. On the other hand, I don't think heaven could come up with a better woman than Lisa. She kept the cabin neat and clean, and she soon learned to cook very well considering what she had to work with. We never had any hard words. She waited on me hand and foot, asking nothing for herself. I guess she spoiled me rotten, but I loved it.

We talked about leaving in the fall before the bad weather hit, but we had our minds made up for us a little sooner than that. The cabin was close to the sawmill and Lisa always brought my lunch, usually sandwiches and a hot soup and coffee. One day in September she was a few minutes late. When she did get there, she was scared. I had never seen her like that, trembling and skittery-eyed, and I didn't understand it. I got scared just looking at her and not knowing what was wrong.

We moved off by ourselves. I started to eat, waiting for her to tell me what was wrong. She couldn't say anything for a minute or so. She seemed frozen. Then it finally came out in a rush of words.

"Rick, a man's been watching the house all morning."

I knew, then, because this was the very thing that had been worrying both of us ever since we'd come here. The lunch bucket was very heavy. I guessed what she'd done before I lifted the jar of soup and package of sandwiches out of the bucket. My gun was in the bottom.

"Where is he?" I asked, slipping the gun under my waistband.

"In the willows," she said. "North of the house."

A small stream ran on the other side of the cabin with a thick fringe of willows on both banks. Between here and where the man was hiding was a scattering of lodgepole pines, too thin for cover, but I'd have to go through them to reach the man.

As soon as I finished eating, I said, "You go to the store and stay there until this is over. If he decided to take you for a hostage, we'd be in a hell of a fix."

She nodded. She kissed me, something she had never done in front of the other men, and walked to the store, carrying my empty lunch bucket. I got up, knocked some dirt off my pants trying to be casual about it, and moved over to where the owner of the sawmill stood talking to another man.

"I'm sick," I said. "I'm going to the cabin."

"You're out of a job if you do," he said. "I didn't hire a man to go off . . ."

I didn't wait to hear the rest of it. I picked up an ax, put it over my shoulder, and started circling through the lodgepoles. I didn't know if the man could see me or not, but in case he could, I kept my head tipped back, staring at the trees as if looking for something in particular. I was banking on the chance that the dry gulcher didn't know me by sight.

I didn't have the slightest doubt about what he was here for. If he'd had an honest purpose, he'd have come to the door and asked for me if I was who he wanted to see. I figured he'd found out at the store which cabin I lived in, and then settled down to wait till I came home.

It took me fifteen minutes or more to get around to where I wanted to be, then I dropped the ax and drew my gun. I started crawling toward the cabin on my hands and knees. Every time I heard a jay or a squirrel or the leaves rustling in the wind, I dropped belly flat and waited, thinking the man might get nervous and start looking around, but I guess he was used to forest noises.

I could see his back plain enough, scrooched down in the willows. I worked up to within fifteen or twenty feet of him, then I said, "You want me, mister?"

I cocked my gun. I'm sure he heard what I said and he had to hear the gun being cocked, but he didn't move for several seconds. He must have been paralyzed by fear, being reasonably sure I was the man he'd come here to kill.

When he did move, he came around fast, his gun in his hand. He never got off a shot. I hit him twice, once in the chest and once in the throat. It looked to me as if blood spurted ten feet. He fell back, but he never quite hit the ground, his body suspended by the willows behind him.

He was dead when I got to him. I took a good, long look at him, but I was sure I had never seen him before. He might have been in the invading army. By this time they had all been turned loose simply because Smith County didn't have the money to try a mob of men, so some of the Texas gunslingers could have been hired to find me and kill me. I hadn't seen all of them that morning at the Circle A, and I wouldn't have remembered their faces if I had.

I didn't tarry but went on through the willows to the cabin. Lisa was running from the store. The men were coming from the sawmill. I went to meet Lisa. She was crying. I took her into my arms and held her and said over and over, "I'm all right," until she quieted down.

When the men got there, I said, "There's a dead man yonder," and jerked my thumb in his direction. "He was trying to ambush me, but I got him first."

"We'll have to hold you for trial," the owner said.

That made me hot. I pushed Lisa away and put my hand on the butt of my gun. I said, "We're leaving pronto. You figure you're man enough to hold me?"

I guess I looked pretty mean and tough. I felt mean and tough. I'd been through too much to be held for weeks in some stinking jail and then tried for defending my life. I made my point. The men walked on past the cabin to the dead man, not saying another word.

We packed up a few things. I saddled the horses, and we were on our way south in a matter of minutes, not even taking time to collect the wages I had coming.

15

WE RODE SOUTH, then crossed the continental divide and turned south again. I started looking for work, but I didn't have any luck until we were over Raton Pass. We heard about a big outfit called the Half Moon east of the town of Raton, so we rode out there just on the off chance I could catch on. I did, though mostly it was Lisa they wanted.

The ranch belonged to a man named Rafael Garcia. His wife, Juanita, was, I think, the most beautiful woman I ever saw in my life. When we showed up, she'd just had a baby. They had an older child, a five-year-old boy. Mrs. Garcia had not been feeling well after having the baby, and they wanted Lisa to take care of the children.

This was a side of Lisa I had not known before. She loved children and they just naturally loved her. At first the arrangement had been a temporary one for a week, then a month, and by that time Mrs. Garcia had become fond of Lisa and asked her to stay permanently.

I don't think they needed another rider, but they gave me a job just to keep Lisa. We had a small but comfortable adobe house about one hundred yards from the big house, close enough to get word to Lisa quickly if they needed her for the children, and far enough away to give us the privacy we wanted.

It was here that I met Ed Vernal. I have never understood what takes place between two people when they first meet. Sometimes I have taken a hearty dislike to people when I first meet them, but more often than not I have a neutral feeling, neither liking nor disliking them, and then on occasion I have met people I took to instantly. It had been that way with Lisa, but it was the same with Ed Vernal.

He was older than I was by ten years or so. He was a better cowhand than I'd ever be, partly because he'd had more experience, but mostly, I think, because he had incredible muscular rhythm and coordination. As a matter of fact, he did anything well that he attempted.

For one thing, he was the best rifle shot I ever ran into. The tall tales you hear about a man being able to shoot the wings off a fly and not touch the body of a fly were almost true with him.

He was also a great reader. He was the only cowboy I ever knew who had a library of his own. When we rode into Raton, the rest of us would light out for a bar, but he would first go to a store that sold books. If he found one he hadn't read, he'd buy it. Then, if he had any money left, he'd look us up and have a drink. He was, he said, an omnivorous reader. It's his word, not mine. I'd never heard of it before.

Originally he had come from the East, Pennsylvania, I believe. He had started to college, but he was the independent kind who never took to discipline, so he quit, left home, and came west. He'd been on the Half Moon for several years. When I first met him, I couldn't help thinking of Al Swan and how different they were. Al could have lived in the West for fifty years, but he'd never have turned out the way Ed had.

I guess Ed took to me the way I took to him. We spent a lot of time together right from the first. Lisa liked him, too, and I'm not surprised that he liked Lisa. I never saw a man who didn't like Lisa. If she'd been the flirty kind, we'd have had trouble, but she never gave me any excuse to be jealous.

Ed spent many an evening with us in our house playing cards or just sitting and talking. Lisa often brought the baby to our place and Ed loved her. He'd hold her while Lisa did the dishes and shake his head and say, "It's a crime the way they grow up, isn't it?"

I didn't agree to that, holding that a woman was of more value than a baby girl, but I guess it's all the way you see things. Ed never was much for women. Some of the men would hit for a whorehouse in Raton when we went to town, but not Ed.

It was surprising that he took to the baby the way he did. He was a cold customer in most ways. He could hide his feelings better than anyone I ever saw, which is one reason he was a hell of a good poker player.

During the summer we often rode into the mountains to the north, taking a lunch along and spending a Sunday afternoon just looking down on the Half Moon buildings and the range that ran on and on as far as we could see. The Garcia boy who was a good rider for a child sometimes went with us, but the Garcias would never let us take the baby.

"A girl's place is in the home," Garcia would say, and that was the end of the discussion.

I thought the months that we'd spent in North Park were close to heaven, but the five years we lived on the Half Moon were a step closer. I didn't know until near the end of those five years that Lisa wanted a baby, but it wasn't our luck to have any. As it turned out, I'm glad we didn't.

One reason that our life was better on the Half Moon than it had been in North Park was the fact that we were far enough from Wyoming to feel safe. As time passed, I began to think the Association had forgotten all about me.

I told Ed about my situation, and he said as long as I stayed out of Wyoming I was probably safe. I believed him because I wanted to. I began to think that we'd live our lives out right here on the Half Moon. Ed wasn't as settled as I was, not having a wife, and I sensed he was beginning to feel restless. He wanted to write about the West and he said he hadn't seen very much of it.

Our bubble was bound to burst, I guess. Ed claims that no man is meant to be as happy as I was, and I suppose he was right. It worried me when I got to thinking about it and I thought I'd like to grab these moments of life and make time stand still because they could never be any better than they were right then, but that's not given to man, either.

The bubble was pricked one Saturday afternoon when I walked into a bar in Raton and saw the Brazos Kid. At first I just stood and stared at him. He was at the far end of the bar. When he saw me, he stared, too. I don't think he knew me for a moment, but I knew him, all right. I'm not as distinctive looking as he was. That narrow, sharp-featured face of his was one I'd never forget.

The part that stunned me was my belief I had killed him in Ellie's backyard in Casper. For a time I just stood there, paralyzed, thinking I must be looking at a ghost or a twin brother, then he apparently recognized me because he wheeled and rushed out through the back door.

I started after him, but the saloon was crowded. I had to elbow my way through the other cowboys who were milling around in the middle of the long run. By the time I got to the alley, he was nowhere in sight.

I hunted all afternoon for the bastard. I looked in all of the saloons and brothels, I checked at the hotels, and finally went to the sheriff's office, but apparently no one else had seen the man. I suppose he had a camp in the mountains north of Raton. He wasn't in town. That was all I knew for sure except for one obvious fact. He was a coward.

He must have come to Raton looking for me, though how he knew I was here was a mystery. Of course he may just have been hunting blind, but I was more inclined to think that someone who knew the Association still wanted my hide had sent word to Wyoming and the Association had given the Kid the job of killing me.

Anyhow, we could have had it out right there face to face, but he didn't have the guts to do it. He'd been brave as all hell that morning at the Circle A when he had Col. Jessup and the rest of the mob on his side. He'd been brave in Ellie's backyard when he expected the deputy to drive me out through the back for him to kill.

Now that he had a chance to earn his bounty money from the Association, he broke and ran. He preferred to dry gulch me. From that moment I was scared, figuring 'he'd be looking for me at night from the mouth of a dark alley or be lying in an arroyo waiting for me to ride by so he could pick me off.

I rode home that afternoon, more uneasy than I had been since I'd left North Park. I didn't tell Lisa what had happened until after supper, but she knew something was wrong. She didn't quiz me, but then she never did. When something was bothering me, she always let me tell it in my own good time.

After supper I told her what had happened, and then said, "Maybe we ought to get out of here. I'm scared. It would be one thing if I could fight him, but just waiting for him to kill me is something else."

She came to me and sat on my lap. She said, "Honey, I don't believe you're scared for yourself. I think you're worried about me."

Sometimes Lisa amazed and shocked me the way she could read my mind. She was dead right. I knew the Brazos Kid hated me. He'd have to after me shooting him in Casper and getting away when he had every advantage on his side. I'd made him look like a fool. He wouldn't be satisfied just shooting me. He'd want to hurt me, and the best way he could do that would be to get at Lisa.

"That's right," I said after I'd thought about it a minute. I didn't know what to say because I didn't want to worry her any more than I had. Finally I added, "I might just as well be dead if he killed you."

She put her fingers over my mouth. "Now hush up that kind of talk. He's not going to kill me. He wouldn't have the courage to come onto a big spread like this to harm me. Sooner or later he'll show up and you'll kill him. I don't want to run anymore, Rick. We like it here. It's going to take more than fear to make me leave."

I felt the same way. She was right, I thought. It was foolish to worry about her. There was always someone here when the crew was gone. The cook and Monte Moran, the old chore man, and Mrs. Garcia and the children. So I ended up by making Lisa promise not to leave the place unless I was with her, or at least someone who could protect her.

That's the way it should have been, but it didn't turn out that way, which proves, I guess, that no matter how carefully you plan something, you can't see all the things that might happen. About a month after Lisa and I had talked about what the Kid might do, everyone except the cook decided to leave the ranch for a day and watch the branding which we were doing a few miles to the south.

I knew what the plan was and that Monte Moran was going to hook up the team to the carriage and Mrs. Garcia and the children and Lisa were going to make a day of it. What I didn't know was that after we left that morning, Lisa sprained her ankle playing with the children and didn't feel like going. She told Mrs. Garcia the cook would be there and she'd make out fine. Mrs. Garcia didn't know about the Brazos Kid, so she never dreamed that Lisa might be in danger.

I was using the branding iron when the carriage rolled in that morning. For a little while I was too busy to look up, and when I did, I couldn't see Lisa. Right then I was sick. I wasn't in the habit of having hunches or seeing visions, but I had something right then, a certainty that froze my insides and told me the worst was going to happen in spite of anything I could do.

I knew that this was exactly what the Brazos Kid would be waiting for if he'd been watching the buildings. I had a feeling he had been. There was plenty of broken country to the north where he could hide and with a pair of good glasses he could see everything that was going on.

I replaced the iron in the fire and said to Ed, "You can have the job for a while." I walked to the carriage, having to hold myself from running. I asked Mrs. Garcia, "Where's Lisa?"

"She's probably in bed," Mrs. Garcia said. "She sprained her ankle and it was hurting her so much she didn't feel like coming. She can't put her weight on . . ."

I didn't hear the rest. I wheeled and ran to my horse and mounted and cracked steel to him. I never pushed a horse so hard in my life. As I approached our house, I saw a black gelding tied in front. A moment later I saw the body of the cook lying face down on the ground about twenty feet from our front door.

I pulled my horse up and swung down and ran toward our front door, my gun in my hand. I wasn't thinking. I was just feeling. I knew damned well what I'd find. The only question was whether I was in time.

The Brazos Kid was so interested in what he was doing, or what he had done, that he didn't know I was there until he heard the pound of my boots on the front room floor. He was in the bedroom standing beside the bed. He whirled toward me, right hand sweeping his gun from leather.

I shot him in the belly and then I shot him again. I walked toward him, shooting until my gun was empty, then I turned to the bed. He had torn all of Elie's clothes off her. She lay on top of the quilts naked. She was dead.

I sat down on the side of the bed and took her into my arms. There were no marks on her. He must have smothered her with a pillow. I rocked back and forth, holding her, and all I could think of in that moment of shock was that I had never married her and I had never told her I loved her.

16

I DON'T KNOW how long I sat there holding Lisa's body in my arms. I lost all track of time, but I remember Ed Vernal coming into the bedroom and laying a hand on my shoulder and saying, "This is no good, Rick. She's gone."

He took her body from me very gently and laid it on the bed and covered it with a blanket, then he took me by the arm. He said, "Let's go outside."

I let him lead me into the front room and then I stiffened and rebelled. I said, "No, I'll stay here."

I jerked loose from his grip and sat down on the black leather couch where we had sat together so many times, my arm around her, her head on my shoulder. Then I began to cry, great violent sobs that shook my whole body. I had never cried like that as a boy even when my stepfather had beaten me.

My memory of what happened the next three days were blurred. I didn't sleep much after the funeral. The Garcias were very kind, taking care of the funeral arrangements and letting Lisa be buried in the family cemetery which was on a small ridge above the house.

I had not thought of my future. I guess I hadn't thought of much of anything, but the evening after the funeral Ed came in and sat down and we smoked and didn't say anything for a long time. Almost everyone who came to the funeral cried, some of them men I didn't think had a tear in their whole body. It proved what I

114

already knew, that everyone who had even a passing acquaintance with Lisa had loved her.

I could not make any sense out of it when I remembered what she had been and where I had found her. I felt guilty then, thinking I had not appreciated her, and yet I knew I had no reason to feel guilty because I had made her happy. I was sure of one thing. No one on the Half Moon would have believed me if I had told them where I had first met Lisa.

After a long time, Ed asked, "What do you figure to do, Rick?"

"I don't know," I answered. "I hadn't even thought about it."

"If you stay here, the Association will send another man to kill you," he said, "now that they know where you are."

"By God, I hope they do," I said. "They can't hurt me now."

"If another dry gulcher shows up," Ed said, "and you're lucky and kill him, you're not accomplishing anything more than cutting off another branch. The roots will stay right where they were."

"Are you telling me I ought to go back to Wyoming and start shooting every member of the Association I can find?"

"Hell no. In the first place you couldn't do it. In the second place, you'd kill some innocent men. I'd think that most of the cowmen who belong to the Association are as decent as anybody. Probably the men who want you dead are the ones who were involved in the invasion and they're doing this on their own. They'd be the ones to shoot if you could find out who they were."

I nodded, knowing that what he said made sense, but at that moment I never wanted to see any part of Wyoming again. I said so, but Ed shook his head.

"That's the way you feel now," he said. "You'll change."

"And what do I do until I change?" I demanded.

"That was what I wanted to talk about," Ed said. "I guess you know I've stayed here about as long as I can.

Fact is, I wouldn't have been here this long if it hadn't been for you. I was waiting for you and Lisa to get tired of living here and I figured we could take off together."

"To where?"

He grinned and shrugged his shoulders. "Anywhere, son. Just anywhere. There's no good reason to stay here. I don't owe the Half Moon or the Garcias or anybody else a damned thing. Neither do you. All I know is that there's a lot of country I haven't seen."

I hadn't guessed that Ed had stayed on the Half Moon waiting for me and Lisa to get tired of living here. Now I thought about what he'd said and I knew he was right. There was nothing to hold me here except Lisa's grave, and although I still didn't know much about heaven, I couldn't believe that the real Lisa I loved was buried up there on that ridge.

"All right," I said. "Let's ride out in the morning."

"Good. How much money do you have?"

Lisa and I had saved a good deal during the five years we had been here. Not that we had ever talked about what we'd do with it. It was just that we hadn't needed much money. Garcia had not charged us anything for the house. He had let us have groceries at the wholesale price he paid in Raton. Lisa was not one to dress extravagantly, partly because there was nowhere to go except to an occasional dance.

I took my time answering because I didn't think it was any of Ed's business. Still, he wasn't one to dig into my business just to satisfy his curiosity, so I said, "A little over one thousand dollars."

"I've got about that much," he said. "It'll keep us going for a while."

"Why did you want to know?"

I wanted to know how soon we'd have to stop and go to work. I'd like to be able to go where we want to and stay as long as we want to and then ride on without having to look for a job. Or if we do go to work, to stay just as long as we feel like it and no longer. I've told you I want to write about the West, and I can't do that until I've seen more if it than I have now."

I didn't think I'd be happy unless I was working. Just riding around seeing the country and sitting on my hind-end wasn't my notion of how to spend the rest of my life, but I could thresh that out with Ed later.

We drew our time the next morning. Ed sold his books to the Garcias and we shook hands and rode west the next day. We turned south and went clear to the Mexican line, and then wandered into Arizona.

I discovered that I could live the way Ed wanted to better than I had thought, but something was happening to me, something I didn't like. I found myself drinking more than I ever had. I always had been one to gravitate into fights if there was one around, but now I was worse. I was starting the fights. Ed talked to me about it, I listened and agreed, and kept on being just as ornery and belligerent as ever.

The following year Ed must have decided that work was what I needed. We drifted north into southeastern Oregon and caught on with a big outfit west of Steens Mountain. Something else had happened to me, too. I had never been one to hate. Sure, I had not liked a lot of people and conditions I'd run into. Maybe I had hated them, but not with the steady ache that twisted my guts into knots the way it was now. It was like rust that takes the edge off a knife. I hated Col. Jessup and Pete Martin and everybody in the Association.

It came on me so slowly I was not entirely aware of it but I must have showed it because Ed sensed what was happening to me. He said, "You're about ready to go back to Wyoming, Rick. You're going to have to work that bile out of your system."

I hadn't thought about it, but I did now and I decided he was right. I wasn't drinking much and I didn't seem to need to fight the way I had right after Lisa's death. I guess my hate was a sort of festering sore and I had to wait for it to come to a head. It hadn't yet.

I shook my head. "I don't think I'm ready yet. Let's take the long way to get to Wyoming. Through Montana. You've never been there."

"That's the long way to get there, all right," Ed said. "No, I've never been there. It's time I went."

That's what we did, taking more than a year. We wound up in Miles City. It hadn't changed much, grown a little, but it was the same cow town I'd known when I threw in with Deuce Taylor and we'd made the hunting trip with Al Swan.

I looked up some men I'd known when I'd been there before. I had a mustache and I looked a hell of a lot older than when I'd left Miles City. I'll admit I hadn't realized how much I'd changed until I had to tell most of these men who I was.

The man who gave me my biggest surprise was the bartender who had been in the hotel bar when Deuce and I took care of the three hardcases. He was tending bar in the Cottage Saloon, and what amazed me was that he recognized me before I figured out who he was.

I'd ordered a drink and was standing at the bar when I noticed him staring at me. Finally he poured my drink and then leaned toward me, asking, "You're Rick Patterson, ain't you? You left here with Deuce Taylor, why, it must have been nine, ten years ago."

I had to look at him before I recognized him. We shook hands and I said, "Yeah, I'm Rick Patterson. I'm surprised you knew me. I didn't even think you knew my name."

"Well, I'll tell you," he said, grinning a little. "I didn't know your name until after you and Deuce handled them three horse thieves. I've seen some good scraps, but that was the damnedest fight I ever seen. In the first place, me or nobody else figured old Deuce had it in him to gut a hardcase like he done. In the second place, you was pretty much a kid and I didn't figure you could take care of yourself the way you done. Yes sir, that was a hell of a fight. You made yourself a quick reputation in this burg."

I didn't know what to say. I'd been in so many fights since then and had my brains jarred loose by so many fists that I had almost forgotten the affair with the horse thieves. I said, "I didn't suppose you'd remember it after all this time, or that you'd recognize me."

"I have a good memory for faces," he said. "The man Deuce gutted died, and the one you cooled off finally died, too. He never got out of jail alive." He scratched his head, and then he said, "If I recollect right, you and Deuce took a greenhorn up the Tongue on a hunting trip. His name was Al Swan or something like that."

"His name was Al Swan," I said. "I've always wondered what he did. He loved this country and talked about buying a ranch. I don't know what he'd do with one if he had it, but when he was with us, he tried to buy one he took a liking to."

The bartender got a smug look on his face about like a tomcat that's been in the cream. He said, "Well now, Mr. Patterson, I'll tell you something you won't believe. He did come back and he bought a ranch in Wyoming. Purty close to Sundance if I remember right. South of the Devil's Tower apiece."

That knocked the wind out of me. I didn't think Al would ever come back, and if he did, I figured his second trip would be like his first one, so I guess I stared at the bartender with my mouth open as if I didn't believe it.

He laughed and held up his right hand. "I ain't lying, Mr. Patterson. So help me, that's exactly what he done. He was around Miles City for a while looking for a place. That was, let's see, four or five years ago. Finally he got wind of this outfit in Wyoming and he went down and looked at it and wound up buying. It's on the Bell Foosh. Fishhook, his brand is."

"How has he made out?"

"He done purty good for a while," the bartender answered. "Better'n most greenhorns do who come out here and go broke in a year or two and then head back for home. I ain't heard lately, but when a cowhand comes in here who's been down in that country, I ask him about Swan. They all say he's having a hard time now. A tough neighbor moved in and is stealing his range. Sometimes you wonder if they have any law down there at all."

I pushed my glass back across the bar for another drink. I didn't have any idea I'd know who the neighbor was, but just for lack of anything better to say, I asked, "You know who the tough neighbor is?"

"Sure do," the bartender said as he poured my drink. "Yes sir, it's one of them bastards who got mixed up in the Smith County ruckus. Say, you was in that, too, wasn't you?"

He was playing with me, I thought. I said, a little curtly, I guess, "Yes, I was mixed up in it. Now who is this tough hand?"

"Fellow named Pete Martin," he said. "Used to be sheriff of Smith County, they tell me, then he went bad and killed some of the little fellers around Grizzly. One of them trigger happy sons of . . ."

I tossed a coin on the bar and walked out, leaving my drink where he had set it. That night I said to Ed, "I'm ready to go back to Wyoming. There's no reason for you to go because I'm probably committing suicide and I don't see any sense in you getting involved in it."

"You probably are committing suicide," Ed said, "but I'll go along anyhow. Fact is, I wouldn't think of doing anything else."

17

WE CAMPED ONE night on the Belle Fourche almost at the foot of the Devil's Tower. I'd been told that the top of it was about 1,200 feet above the river and I could believe it. Most of it was straight up. It reminded me of a giant thumb pointed straight at the sky. We'd seen it for miles ahead of us, and now we were here beside it.

I lay on my back, my head on my saddle, and stared at the pillar of rock. I wondered if anyone had ever climbed it and decided not, that it couldn't be climbed by a human being. I also wondered what was on top of it.

When I saw something like this, I always had a crazy idea that there might be a city up there that none of us down here had ever seen. The top looked as if it might be reasonably level. Perhaps the city was populated by strange creatures who had wings and could fly.

I expected Ed to laugh when I told him that, but he didn't. He said, "It's ideas like that that start a legend or a myth. Look at those fluted sides. See the grooves? There's an old Indian legend that goes like this.

"Once upon a time there were four young Indian brothers. One of them had a beautiful young wife. The problem was that a great bear had fallen in love with the wife. In order to escape him, the four brothers and the wife climbed to the top of the tower. The bear tracked them and tried to jump to the top, but he never quite made it. Each time that he fell back, his claws made long gashes in the rock. That's how the grooves got there. The youngest brother had the greatest medicine. He had four arrows. He shot them at the bear and the last one struck home and killed the monster, then the brothers and the young wife came back down and lived happy ever after."

"All I've got to say is that the Indians had a better imagination than I have," I said.

"Oh, I don't know about that," Ed said. "Maybe your people don't have wings, but can still fly. It could be that they're the same kind of creatures as the four Indian braves and the young wife. How did they get to the top and back down again without flying?"

"Don't ask me," I said. "It's your story."

Ed laughed and filled his pipe, then looked at me. "Just what do you figure to do when you get to Swan's ranch?"

"Shake hands with him," I said.

"Oh hell," Ed said in disgust. "You know what I mean. You came here to kill Pete Martin. You're pretty handy with a gun. I suppose he is, too, with a reputation like he's got. You going to ride over there and tell him to go for his gun?"

"That's about what I'll do," I said, "and I'll be doing Al a favor to boot. Just one thing. You stay out of it. This is my show and I aim to play it my way."

"Oh, I'll stay out of it," Ed said. "I'm not one to commit suicide. I've got a lot of things to do before I die."

"So have I," I said, "if I live. I figured Al would put us up for a while. Maybe you could go to work for him."

"You're not?"

"I didn't figure on it," I said. "I want to be free to move around any time and anywhere I want to."

I hadn't figured out exactly what I would do. The one thing I didn't want to do was to tangle with Martin's crew. My first job was to find out a time when I could brace Martin alone. I didn't go into that with Ed because I was determined to play it my way and not have to make excuses to anyone or explain anything.

Ed let it drop at that. He said, "We ought to be there tomorrow, hadn't we?"

"I don't know how far it is from the tower," I said. "The bartender just said it was on the other side. It's on the river, so if we follow it, I guess we'll get there."

We did, late in the afternoon. I was surprised to see as pretty a layout as I ever saw in my life. The house was a big one, the main part constructed of rock, with two wings made of logs. There were a number of buildings and corrals, all in perfect condition, the barn and most of the outbuildings painted red. The board fence that surrounded the house and some of the buildings was painted white. A big arch over the end of the lane held the word FISHHOOK, and below it in smaller letters the words, AL SWAN.

There must have been two hundred acres or more of meadow land that was irrigated from the river. Al had just cut and stacked the hay, and from the number of stacks, it was plain that he'd had a good crop.

Several ridges ran down to the river from the mountains with a scattering of pine timber on them. It looked to me as if he had all the range a man could use. The grass looked good, and if there was another hard winter as there had been the year of the Big Die, Al had plenty of hay.

"A man couldn't ask for anything more," Ed said. "Your friend is either smart or lucky for an Easterner."

"Both, maybe," I said. "I knew he was smart enough if he just had somebody to teach him. He'll learn fast."

"Learning's not enough," Ed said. "He's got to have the guts to hold what he's got."

"I don't know if he has that or not," I said. "He's got to show it."

We turned from the river and rode up the lane that led to the house. A white, board fence lined both sides of the lane. I wondered how much Al had done since he'd bought the ranch. An old time westerner wasn't likely to build white board fences as extensively as Al had, but then maybe he'd bought from another Easterner.

When we rode into the yard Al was standing beside one of the corrals talking to a man who was holding a big bay gelding. He hadn't changed much, a little leaner and more angular than ever if that was possible, and darkly tanned.

He glanced at us, said something more to the man holding the horse, then turned to us. I stepped down, calling, "How are you, Al?"

He stopped about ten feet from me and stared, then he

recognized me and bellowed, "Patterson! Rick Patterson! Where in the hell did you drop from?"

I stepped forward and he came at me in a rush, his hand extended. He gripped my hand and slapped me on the back with the other, then he demanded, "How'd you know I was here?"

"I heard it in Miles City," I said. "This is Ed Vernal. Ed, meet Swan. Ed's looking for a job and I'm riding the grub line."

Al shook hands with Ed, making a quick study of him. "I could use a good man," he said slowly. "A good fighting man. I never thought I'd say those words, Rick, but I'm saying them now because I'm damned desperate." He turned to me. "Did they tell you about that in Miles City?"

"I heard that Pete Martin had moved in beside you and was giving you trouble," I said.

"He's giving me more than trouble," Al said bitterly. "I'll tell you about it after supper." He looked at Ed again, then he asked, "You want a job under those circumstances?"

"You bet I do," Ed said. "I'm not doing any bragging about how much of a fighting man I am, but I'm not afraid of the job."

"Good," Al said. "I'll go tell my wife to put on a couple more steaks. Put your horses up and come on in. Zack," he called to the man with the bay gelding, "give them a hand."

Al wheeled and walked toward the house. I stared at his back for a moment, wondering if this really was the same Al Swan who had gone on the hunting trip with Deuce and me. He wasn't wearing a gun, but he looked the part of a cattleman, even walked like one. I almost thought his legs were bowed.

When we went into the house, Al introduced us to his son Ross who was about eleven, I guess, then to his wife Angela who gave us a quick greeting and immediately returned to the kitchen. She was, I assumed, the same wife he'd had ten years ago and she'd had to get used to the West even more than Al because she had never been out here, but judging from the way she got around in the kitchen, she had made the shift.

I had a feeling that all three of the Swans were happy. Worried, but still happy. I was reminded of the Mrs. Holmes we had met on our hunting trip who had come from New Jersey. She had admitted she had problems, but she'd said she would never go back to New Jersey. I had a hunch Mrs. Swan would say much the same thing.

The boy Ross was a knot-headed kid with freckles and hair that pointed every which way, a typical boy, I thought, who had been young enough when he'd come to Fishhook to grow up as a westerner if his dad survived that long. He was sprawled in front of the fireplace on a bear rug with a book in front of him. He shook hands with us and returned to his reading.

"He's working on *The Spy*," Al said. "It's a tough book for a boy his age, but he's doing fine."

"I read it when I was a kid," Ed said. "I remember I had a hard time with it."

"I should tell you one thing about Ed before you hire him," I said. "He's a bookworm."

Al grinned. "I can overlook that."

"How'd you come to make this jump out here from Rhode Island?" I asked.

Al sighed. "I knew you'd ask that. It's simple enough. When I went back to Rhode Island after the hunting trip, I discovered I could hardly breathe. Too many people. I put up with it for several years, but my wife knew I wasn't going to be able to stay. I would have pulled out before I did, but my father was poorly, so I hung on till he died. My sister and I agreed that we weren't going to stay there, so we sold everything. Angela and Ross decided they could live out here, so we took the train to Miles City figuring we'd take a whack at ranching. This was the first place I saw that I liked, so we bought it."

"Did you put up all that white fence?" I asked.

"I sure did," he said, "and I'm proud of it. I don't give a damn what you or anybody else thinks. To me it sets a ranch off."

"It does for a fact," I said.

He glared at me, getting a little hot, then he shrugged. "Go ahead and hooraw me," he said. "I do what I like out here whether anybody else likes it or not. That was one of the things I noticed when I was here the first time." He rose and, walking to the mantle, picked his pipe up and began filling it. "What happened to Deuce?"

"I don't know," I said. "I doubt that anybody knows except the sons of bitches like your neighbor Martin who were involved in the Smith County war."

"I heard you were in that, too," he said. "Inadvertently, I suppose, though I don't know how much was truth and how much was newspaper lies. Tell me about it."

I told him, making it brief and not mentioning Lisa and calling Ellie's Pleasure Palace a boardinghouse, with Ross being right there with us. Al nodded, then he said, "This is hard for me to understand. I refuse to accept it, though whether I'll live long enough to work at any change is a question. How a small group of men can control the politics of this state the way they do is beyond me. I'm a bigger cattleman than some of them, but I'm an outsider. It's mostly that I don't play by their rules, I guess."

Mrs. Swan called us to supper. It was a good meal and I congratulated her. She smiled and said, "For a transplanted Rhode Islander I think I do pretty well, but we have a beautiful place to live. If Al had bought somewhere else . . ." She shrugged. "Well, I don't think I could have survived."

"She does real well," Al said. "I couldn't ask for a better wife."

"Thank you, kind sir," she said, bowing in his direction.

Al rose. "Let's go to my office," he said.

He led the way down a hall to a room in the west wing. His office was much like similar rooms in other ranch houses I'd seen with its accumulation of guns and ropes and saddles and tally books, but there was a neatness about it that wasn't like the average ranch office. Everything seemed to be in its proper place.

He motioned to two rawhide-bottom chairs and dropped into a swivel chair back of his desk. I asked, "Al, did you ever find that old buffalo bull you used to look for?"

He grinned and said, "If you bastards had told me the truth, I could have quit dreaming about him right then. No, I never found him."

"Go ahead," I said. "Tell us about this ruckus with Martin."

"There's nothing to tell except that he's stealing my range," he said.

"I'm surprised he ever came into enough money to buy an outfit," I said.

"It was Col. Jessup," Al said. "He sold his holdings in Smith County after the trouble there and bought a spread on the Sweetwater, but he was getting old and too bunged up to run a ranch. Martin was his foreman and I guess wormed his way into Jessup's confidence. Some say he stole the old man blind, but I don't know as to that. Anyhow, Jessup sold out, retired to Cheyenne, and loaned Martin enough to buy this spread that's next to mine."

Al knocked his pipe out and filled it again. "The part that gets under my hide is that I can't get the law to do anything. I've got to prove what Martin does, the sheriff says. I've had cattle shot. Fence ripped out. Two men murdered. It's got to be Martin because I had no trouble until he showed up, but I can't prove a thing. The sheriff comes out, looks around, and doesn't find anything."

Al got up, walked to the window, and stared moodily at the meadow below the house that sloped down toward the river. "He's pushing his cattle onto my range a little farther all the time. Now I'm having trouble keeping a crew. Nobody wants to tangle with Martin, knowing his reputation as a killer. I suppose that's really the sheriff's trouble. He's afraid of Martin."

"He's got reason to be," Ed said. "Everybody knows his reputation."

Al nodded. "The truth is folks expect me to strap on a gun and go after Martin. Well, he'd kill me. I came out here to have a free life and I'm willing to spend my money and work like hell, but fighting a man like Pete Martin is something I can't and won't do. I'm not one to hire a crew of gunslingers, either, though that's what Martin's done."

"Don't do it," I said. "Don't let what anybody else thinks push you into a fight. You've got your wife and boy to think about."

"I'm not forgetting it," Al said sharply. "I've still got plenty of money. I could sell out here and move to Cheyenne or Denver and make a living with some kind of business, but damn it, I like it here. I shouldn't have to do it. What does a man do in these circumstances, Rick? You've lived in the West all of your life. There must be some answer that's decent and honorable and within the law."

"I'll have to think about it," I said. "Have you got a good pair of glasses?"

"Yes, but what's that got to do with it?"

"Can I borrow them?"

He glared at me, irritated because I was dragging something in that seemed to him to be irrelevent and have nothing to do with his problem. He finally set down at his desk and pulled a drawer open. Lifting the glasses out, he handed them to me. I walked to the window, put the glasses to my eyes and focused them on the horses in the corral, then on the willows along the river. They were good ones that brought out the details of the brush better than any I could afford to buy.

"I'd like to borrow them, Al," I said. "It's time I told you the reason I came here. It's to kill Pete Martin."

18

IF THIS HAD not been a life and death business, the expression on Al's face would have been comical. At first he simply stared at me as if he could not comprehend what I had just said, then the corners of his mouth began to quiver. He asked, in a low tone, "You doing this on account of me?"

"Partly," I said. "I'd like to see you get a chance and you won't have it as long as Pete Martin's gnawing at your range. Mostly it's because Martin was with the invaders, along with being a murderer who gunned down at least two and maybe more young men who were on the side of the small ranchers. I can't kill all the men who were in the mob. Some are gone. Some are dead. But Martin was one of the worst and I aim to execute him."

"You'll put the fear of God into any of the others who are still alive," Ed said.

"I hope so," I said. "I've got a hunch that living and being afraid every minute of your life that somebody was fixing to kill you would be hell."

I knew what I was talking about because I'd been through it in North Park and in New Mexico after I'd seen the Brazos Kid in Raton. I don't think I scared as easily as the mob members who still lived in Wyoming because they must feel guilty for what they had done, but it had been bad enough for me, mostly the constant threat of a dry gulcher catching me in his sights. That's one kind of danger a man can't fight.

"How do you intend to go at this?" Al asked. "Don't

forget that he's got five or six men in his crew and they're a tough lot."

"First I want you to draw me a map of the country around here," I said, "particularly where Martin's spread is. I'll spy on it for a while and that's when I'll decide what to do. I'm not crazy enough to tackle his crew. What I'll try to do is to find him alone."

"He's like a rabid dog," Al said. "Aren't you afraid to face him?"

"No," I said. "I think his reputation is bigger than he is. You'll remember that his killings in Smith County were all bushwhacking jobs. I have no respect whatever for that kind of man. The only danger I'll face is the risk of running into his crew and getting pinned down. If that happens, I'll want some help."

"You'll get it if I know it's happening," he said.

"One more thing," I said. "I'll probably play a little cat-and-mouse game with him just to scare them, though I'm not sure about that yet. If I do, I might wind up leading them here. How many men do you have?"

"Four," he answered. "Five with Ed. Six with me. I wouldn't like it because of Angela and Ross, but if it happens, we'll fight them off. No blame on you, either."

"Good," I said. "Now I'm going to roll in. Have that map ready for me in the morning."

We slept in the bunkhouse that night and ate with the crew the next morning. They weren't what I'd call fighting men, and they looked Ed and me over with considerable care. I had the feeling they were uneasy about us and not a friendly lot, but I hadn't come here to make friends. They were all middle-aged, good cowboys as far as savvy went, but somehow I had the notion that they had lost their will to fight somewhere back along the years.

Ed rode out with them that morning and I went to the house. Al brought the map to me immediately. He said, "I'm not a cartographer, but maybe you can make it out."

I sat down and studied it for several minutes. It showed Martin's ranch, the Rafter M, about four or five miles upstream from Fishhook. It was west of the river half a mile or more in a small valley with a creek flowing past the house and running into the Belle Fourche below the ranch buildings. Apparently he irrigated his hay meadows from this stream. Rocky and timbered ridges lay on both sides of the meadows.

"How far are these ridges from the house?" I asked.

"Not far," he said. "It's a narrow valley. From the top of the ridges you're looking right down on the buildings and corrals." He scratched his chin thoughtfully, then he went on in a low tone, "I see what you've got in mind. I don't know why I didn't think of it."

"I'm not sure it's what I'll do," I said, "but it's an idea."

Mrs. Swan had come into the room. I didn't know she was there until she said, "Mr. Patterson, I suppose there's not any way to stop you from going ahead with this mad scheme. I am fully aware that you are fond of Al and you want to help him. I am also aware that Pete Martin deserves killing and it would bring peace back to us if he were dead, but I cannot countenance this going out to murder a man."

"I won't murder him, Mrs. Swan," I said. "I promise that. He'll have a chance for his gun which is more than he gave the men he killed in Smith County."

She shook her head. "It's a small difference. You'll shoot and kill him whether he has a chance for his gun or not. It's not . . . decent."

"No, it's not," I agreed, "but we haven't reached the place yet where our problems can be solved in a decent way."

Then she lost her temper, and she lashed out angrily, "Don't do this for us, Mr. Patterson."

"I'm not doing it for you," I said. "I haven't given you the real reason I'm doing it."

I told her about Lisa, talking as if she had been my wife which she had been except for the legal technicality the state requires. I finished by saying, "I cannot tell you what it meant to me to lose her. I never realized how much I loved her until she was gone. Pete Martin may have been the one who sent the Brazos Kid after me. It would be like him.

"Whether he did or not, he's like the others who were members of the mob. He wants me dead. All of them do. I know too much, and sooner or later I'll tell or write what I know. These are so-called respectable men, Mrs. Swan. The publicity has died down and they don't want it started again. If Pete Martin knew I was here, he'd be after me with his whole crew. Today! You'd all be in danger on account of me."

I stuffed the map into my pocket and rose and walked out of the house. I hadn't talked about Lisa to anyone for a long time. Now I was remembering. I had tried to forget, tried to put the memory of her into the back of my mind.

I had suffered too much, and now, with Lisa's sweet face and the picture of her in my arms that day as I sat beside her bed flooding my mind, well, I came damned close to crying as I saddled my horse.

My first move was to turn into the hills. When I was above the Rafter M I rode down toward it until I was close enough to run some risk of being seen. I dismounted, left my horse in a close-growing patch of pines, and eased along the ridge until I could look directly down upon the buildings. I brought my Winchester, my canteen, and Al's glasses and settled down to watch, the sun pouring down on me from an absolutely clear sky.

I learned very little that day. The ranch was not much of an outfit compared to Fishhook. It was a man's spread with none of the feminine refinements that a woman brings to a ranch. Obviously no woman was around. The main house was little more than a log cabin of maybe three rooms. In addition there was a variety of other buildings: cookshack, bunkhouse, sheds, and a number of corrals.

As I studied the place through the glasses I had the impression that the Rafter M was rundown. I couldn't imagine Martin really working at running a ranch. I'd run into a number of men like him who were just a little higher on the scale of human values than the Brazos Kid, but they were still hired gun hands, men who were too lazy to work for a living, but weren't above taking a man's life in any manner that was safe for them. I didn't figure Martin was any different from the others.

As I sat there among the rocks with the sun slugging me with a temperature that must have been well over one hundred degrees, the thought occurred to me that Martin never intended to operate this spread as a cattle ranch. Maybe he meant to make it so tough on Al that he'd sell out for a song. Martin could throw the two outfits together and have the kind of big ranch that would appeal to an Easterner, someone like Al who had come west looking for an investment opportunity.

Regardless of Martin's reasoning, his intentions seemed plain enough. I toyed with several ideas. The one that appealed to me the most was to shoot the place up. A man was down there. I didn't remember what Martin looked like, having seen him only once back of Coleman's and Springer's barn with the rest of the invaders, so I wasn't sure whether the man I saw was Martin or not, but I assumed he was. If he'd been any kind of hired hand, he'd have gone out with the crew.

Several times during the morning the man left the house to go to one of the sheds or the cookshack. If it was Martin, I could have a fine time shooting out the windows of the house and cookshack, or maybe dropping a few slugs in front of him as he was walking from one building to another.

I laughed out loud when I pictured Martin dropping flat on his belly and scrambling through the dust of the yard toward the nearest shelter. Or I could wait until the crew came in and trigger shots at them, maybe sting a horse or two and lay the bullets at the men's feet so close they'd be jumping sideways.

The prospect was inviting any way I looked at it. It was what Al knew I meant when I'd asked him how close the rocks were to the ranch buildings, something he could have done. But Al didn't work that way and he never would have done it, though he could have got it through Martin's skull that the harassment game worked both ways. Al could not, I thought, be as tough as life out here demanded.

It didn't take much thought to convince me that I couldn't do anything of the sort because I would destroy my most valuable asset: surprise. So, as alluring as the idea was, I gave it up, knowing that the best thing I could do was simply to ride in and brace Pete Martin. Whatever chance I had of getting him alone would be gone if I gave myself away too soon.

For three days I lay among the rocks, sweating and wiping my face with my bandanna and pulling on my canteen. By the end of the third day I had a good idea of the procedure on the Rafter M. Martin never left the ranch in the mornings. I judged that no one else was there except the cook. The crew rode out usually about the time I reached the rocks and returned late in the afternoon.

The evening of the third day I told Ed I was ready to make my move. I was going alone, I'd shoot it out with Martin, and be on my way. I told him I knew I'd open up the old chase again and they'd hound me as long as I was in Wyoming and longer if they knew where I was, so I'd bust the breeze getting out of the state. There was a good chance they wouldn't find me, at least not until I wanted them to.

"All right," Ed said. "You can do the job. If I was a betting man, I'd lay my money on you."

"If you were a betting man," I said. "Offhand I can't think of more of a betting man than you after all the poker games I've seen you sit in."

"Well then, let's say if I had anybody to bet with," Ed said. "Anyhow, you write to me as soon as you get settled and I'll find you. I'll stay here till then."

"Good," I said. "I'll let you know. Right now don't say anything to Al."

The next morning Ed rode out with the crew. I didn't shake hands with him or do anything which might show this could very well be the last time I'd ever see him. I left Al's glasses in the bunkhouse, then took my time saddling my horse and filling my canteen. I didn't want to reach the Rafter M until the crew was gone. Just as I mounted, Al called to me and left the house, crossing the yard to where I sat my saddle.

He was upset. I had never seen him this way before. He couldn't look at me. Instead, he looked past me as he dug a boot toe into the dust. He said, "Rick, I hate like hell to say this, but the missus, well, she's just not used to the idea of killing a man no matter what he is or has been, so she thinks, well, I mean . . ."

He didn't have the guts to finish what he had started to say. "I savvy," I said. "She wants me to ride out of here and stay out."

"That's about the size of it," he said uneasily. "She hasn't slept since the first morning when you said Martin's wolf pack might chase you here. She's afraid we'll be burned out and her and Ross killed. She says that up till now we haven't done anything to make him strike at us."

"But he's been striking at you," I said. "He'll keep striking harder until you either hit back or move out."

"I reckon that's right," Al said grimly, "but I've got to live with Angela. It's not that she doesn't like you. We've been arguing about it ever since you got here and she's got me worn down to a nubbin."

I leaned forward in the saddle, not sore at Al, but thinking that both of them were mighty damned ungrateful. I said, "Al, your wife is a fine woman, but it looks to me like she's not going to be able to live out here. You're bound to have violence of one kind or another. It's part of the price you pay for living here. Either way, you'd better get your knife out and cut the apron string."

I rode away, leaving Al Swan standing there staring at my back, stripped of his manhood and his pride. I was sorry I had said it. I was sorry about something else. He had promised that if I ran into the crew and got pinned down, he'd bring his men and help me out. I knew now it was an empty promise. I was strictly on my own.

19

I RODE DOWN the lane slowly to the road and turned south, watching for the Rafter M crew. None of them would know me, so I wouldn't have any trouble with them, but if they were close enough to hear shooting, they'd come back in a hurry. Usually they crossed the river east of the buildings, and they should be out of sight and earshot by now.

If they hadn't left, I'd have a problem. All I could do would be to say I was looking for a job. If Martin gave me one, I'd still be in trouble because working for him would be the last thing I wanted. If he said no, which he probably would, then I'd have to ride off and figure some other way to get at him.

As it turned out, I had no reason to worry because the crew was gone. I rode up to the house, seeing no evidence of life except the thin column of smoke rising from the cookshack's chimney. The morning was cooler than the previous ones had been and there was not even a breath of wind. Several horses in the corral noticed my approach and stood watching, their ears up. A mongrel dog that had been sleeping in front of the house got to his feet when he saw me and growled, showing ugly, yellow teeth.

I dismounted and stood with my horse between me and the cookshack in case the cook decided to take a shot at me. I called, "Martin."

Nothing happened for a moment except that the dog started to bark. I yelled again, "Martin."

This brought him to the door. He bellowed at the dog,

"Shut up, Nero." He pushed the screen back and stepped through the door. He asked in a surly tone, "What do you want?"

"You," I said. "I want to talk to you."

"Go ahead and talk," he said. "I don't have anything to talk to you about."

"Yes you do," I said. "You don't know it, but you do."

For a terrible moment I thought he was going to refuse to come closer. If he had wheeled back into the house, I would have shot him in the back. Now that I was this close to doing what I had come for, I had no intention of failing.

Maybe it was curiosity, or maybe he was afraid to turn his back to me. I have no way of knowing. In any case, he stepped off the porch and walked toward me. He was tall and slender with a face almost as sharp-featured as the Brazos Kid's had been. He reminded me of a wolf more than any other man I had ever seen, partly because of his sharp features and partly because of his walk. It's hard to describe his walk, but slithering comes close, or maybe creepy.

I had thought of the Brazos Kid as looking like a coyote, but I gave Martin a little more credit and compared him to a wolf. I thought I read contempt in his face, and I thought I smelled evil about the man, but this was probably only my imagination because I knew what he had done.

He stopped twenty feet from me. "What's this all about? I've got work to do and I don't have time to talk to every saddle tramp who comes by."

I was right about the contempt, and evil was in him whether I smelled it or not. I said, "You don't recognize me, do you?"

He scowled and shook his head, "Why should I?"

"It's been a long time," I said. "The last time and I guess the only time you ever saw me was behind Coleman's and Springer's barn. I was with Deuce Taylor. What happened to him?"

"Rick Patterson!" The words were jolted out of him.

The contempt was gone and now I sensed fear in him. "What do you want with me?"

"A killer showed up in North Park in Colorado who was fixing to kill me," I said. "Did you send him?"

"Hell no."

He backed up a step, his gaze flicking to one side and then the other as if trying to see some way to get out of a trap. He'd been lured out here and now he was wishing he was somewhere else.

"The Brazos Kid tried to kill me in Casper," I said. "I shot him and thought he was dead, but later on he showed up in New Mexico still trying to kill me. I won't make the same mistake with you."

For just a moment the shadow of death was on his face. Now he looked more like a wolf than ever, a cornered wolf. His right hand was close to the butt of his gun. He took another step back and then he made his try. He was slow, slower even than I had expected him to be and I had been reasonably sure that any man who murdered from the safety of a hiding place would not be fast with his gun.

I gave him time to pull his Colt from leather and then I shot him. He was slammed back against the hitch pole by the impact of the heavy slug, his gun going off, a wild shot that missed me by ten feet. He sagged there against the hitch pole for a moment, hanging like a piece of wet wash.

I shot him again and this time he slipped off the hitch pole and spilled out full length on the ground, his arms flung out in the grotesque manner of a scarecrow that has been lifted from its resting place in a garden and flung to one side.

I walked to him and picked up his gun and threw it as far as I could. I looked down at him; I saw the red bubbles of blood at the corners of his mouth, and I thought of Coleman and Springer, and I thought of the times he had hidden beside lonely roads in Smith County and shot young men in the back who had never done him any harm and were only trying to carve a living for their wives and children from a wild land.

He was dead. I made sure of that before I turned back to my horse. I had no more feeling for him than I would have had for a wolf that had tried to kill me. Just as I swung into my saddle, the cook cut loose from the cook-shack, so I hastened my departure. It was my luck that the cook was a bad shot. A short time later I was out of range and the cook didn't waste any more ammunition.

I arrived in Sundance late that afternoon. The first thing I did was to buy supplies which I tied behind my saddle, then I looked the sheriff up. He was too old and fat for his job, and I could understand why Al had failed to get any action from him.

"I'm Rick Patterson," I said. "I shot and killed Pete Martin this morning. It was a fair fight. He had plenty of chance to draw."

He was uneasy the moment I mentioned my name. Apparently I had a bigger reputation in Wyoming than I had realized. He said, "Well, as long as it was a fair fight, I reckon I've got no cause to hold you."

"I thought I ought to report it," I said.

He nodded. "I'm glad you did. I'll go out in the morning and see about it."

"All right, then I'll be moseying along," I said and, mounting, rode out of town.

I took a westerly route across the state, avoiding towns and stopping now and then at a ranch for a meal. I shot an antelope which kept me in meat for several days. People that I passed on the road paid no more attention to me than the usual "Howdy" as they rode by. I figured the sheriff would see to it that the news about me killing Pete Martin got around, but now I began to wonder if he had. I didn't get a chance to look at a newspaper, so I don't know whether the shooting was in any of them or not.

If I had known that any of the invaders lived in the country I rode through I would have stopped and called on them, but the only one I'd heard about was Col. Jessup in Cheyenne, and I didn't get anywhere near Cheyenne. Besides, I had no intention of wasting my time on a senile old man.

What I hoped, of course, was that the survivors would

hear about the Martin killing and figure their time was next. I didn't really care whether I killed any of them or not, but I hoped they all died of fright. I knew that was day dreaming. Still, I kept telling myself that to live day after day under the constant threat of death was to my way of thinking a worse fate than being killed outright.

I had not been alone like this for a long time. Funny, but I had not realized how close I had been with Ed Vernal through the years after Lisa's death. It felt good to be alone. I had plenty of time to think, but the result of my thinking wasn't very good. I had reached a point where I didn't really care whether I lived or not.

As long as Lisa had been alive, I'd had a purpose in living. Simply having someone to love and being loved was enough to give purpose to my life, particularly since love had been a missing element in my life up to the time I met Lisa. Recently, of course, I'd had a driving desire for revenge, but now that didn't seem very important. The fact that Pete Martin deserved to die was beside the point. Killing him just hadn't given me any real satisfaction.

I thought about death during those long days in the saddle and at night beside my campfire more than I ever had. The more I thought about it, the less value I saw in life. I would never find another woman I wanted and I would never settle down again and have a home and family which is what a normal man would do.

I was marked for death and I would be hounded by the Association as long as I lived. I honestly didn't think I could ride far enough to escape them. These men had money, and they would spend it so they could live their last years without worrying about me.

The part that bothered me the most about dying was the manner in which I would do it. I didn't care if someone shot me and I died quick and sudden, but I had a horrible fear of drowning or hanging. Dying from a lingering disease of some kind also terrified me. If I ever was forced into a corner from which there was no escape, I'd shoot myself.

When I reached Casper, I rode through town as bold as brass, thinking that if anyone wanted me he could have me if he was man enough to do the job. It was unlikely that anyone would recognize me even if he had seen me before. Anyhow, I guess I was a free man for the first time in years. I quit worrying about myself.

I stopped at the post office and wrote a card to Ed telling him I was safe and healthy and that I'd head the next day for Elk City. Then I looked up Ellie's Pleasure Palace. I was surprised and disappointed. The house had gone to pot. The yard was covered by weeds a foot high, the gate in front sagged, being held by one hinge, the house needed painting, and even some of the shingles were gone from the roof.

Ellie came to the door in answer to my ring. She was fatter than ever. She had gone to pot about as bad as her house. She wore a long, dirty kimono, her hair looked as if it hadn't been brushed or combed for weeks and resembled a rat's nest, and she was dirty. Even though she stood five feet from me I could smell her. She stunk. For all of her fat when I had stayed here, she had always kept herself clean and decent and therefore reasonably attractive.

She stared at me as if I was a complete stranger. I thought she'd recognize me, but she didn't. She said, "I ain't in business no more so you might as well go somewhere else."

"I'm not here for business," I said. "I'm Rick Patterson."

I thought she'd welcome me, but she didn't. She started cursing me and calling me a thief. "You stole my best girl and my horse and all the money I had in the house," she screamed, "and you never paid me for the gun I gave you. I took you in and gave you a place to hide where you'd be safe and that was your way of thanking me. I'm going to call a policeman. I lost my girls after you took Lisa because we didn't have enough business. She was my drawing card and you stole her."

She knew words that no self-respecting mule skinner would ever use. I had no intention of standing there and listening to that, so I drew one hundred dollars out of my pocket. I handed her the money, saying, "That'll pay you for your old mare and the gun and the money we took."

Her face lighted up as she counted the money. I walked to my horse, mounted, and rode out of town. I wished I had just mailed the money to her.

20

I'VE SAT HERE in my cell for weeks and written about the things that have happened to me since I was fourteen. I've thought about them, too. One point is clear. I do not know all the facts that brought about my arrest for the murder of young David Lamond. I know the whys and whats of everything else that has happened to me better than I do these that occurred near Elk City. I can only guess at the truth.

It took me two days of riding across country to reach Elk City. I topped a high ridge and looked down on the town in late afternoon, figuring that I was still about an hour away. I had intended to stay there overnight and then take off the next morning for Utah.

I dropped down off the ridge, crossed a small gulch, and started climbing a smaller ridge when I heard two shots from the other side. I didn't think much about them right then, figuring it was just somebody hunting, but after I topped the ridge, I saw the wounded boy lying at the foot of a tall rock upthrust.

I reined up and dismounted. The boy was unconscious. He had a thigh wound and had lost a lot of blood. I had a feeling he was mighty near death and I couldn't do anything for him. His pulse was very slow. So feeble, in fact, I had trouble finding it. I said something to him, but he was too far gone to answer me. I thought my voice might rouse him, but I don't think he heard me.

I took my knife out of my pocket and slit his pants leg, thinking I could put a tourniquet above the wound, but he

143

died before I finished it. I got to my feet and looked down at the boy's body, thinking I didn't know where he belonged or what his name was or anything of the sort. I didn't see his horse. I didn't want to go off and leave his body there, but I didn't know what else to do.

That was when John Ash said from somewhere behind me, "I've got you dead to rights, mister. You make one fast move for your gun and I'll blow your backbone apart. Now hook the moon and turn around, slow."

I obeyed and saw John Ash. He was holding a gun on me and wore a star on his shirt. It's funny how some faces don't register on your mind, but there are others you remember. Ash had the kind of face I couldn't forget with a chin that stuck out and a sharp nose that hung down till it seemed they almost met. He also had a strawberry splotch on his right cheek just below his eye.

Ash had probably changed his name, something I had too much pride to do, so I know I can't prove this, but I know damned well he was standing beside Pete Martin that morning when the invaders caught me behind Coleman's and Springer's barn. It isn't a coincidence that I'd run into him here, with him packing a star because the Association didn't want any of the gunmen they'd hired for the invasion to get unhappy enough to talk, so a good many of them had been hired as lawmen. If I hadn't run into Ash, I'd probably have run into some of the others.

Before I thought, I blurted, "Say, you were one of the invaders, weren't you?"

That question made him mighty jumpy. I'm sure he didn't recognize me then, though he may have made a good guess because I think he had the word from the Sundance sheriff that I'd shot Pete Martin and to keep an eye open for me.

"Hell no," he said. "Who are you?"

About that time I realized I'd been stupid and had made a bad mistake. If he found out for sure who I was, he'd probably cut me down right here, so all I could do was to play cute. I knew he'd find out my identity sooner or later, but right now I was working to stay alive until I got to the Elk City jail.

"My name's John Smith," I said. "I figured on riding into Elk City tonight and going on tomorrow to Utah."

"Mister, you ain't going nowhere," Ash said. "It's lucky I came over the top of the ridge in time to see you shoot Davey Lamond."

I thought he might try to hold me for Pete Martin's killing, but I hadn't expected this. For a moment I couldn't think of anything to say. I just stood and stared. Later I wished I'd made a try for my gun. He'd have killed me, but it would have been better than hanging.

Finally I got my tongue to working and I said, "By God, I didn't shoot him and you didn't ride over the ridge in time to see anything of the kind. You'll find out my Winchester hasn't been fired if you'll look at it."

He backed up to my horse, still holding his gun on me, and pulled my rifle from the scabbard. He eared back the hammer and fired into the air twice, then slipped the Winchester back into the boot.

He said blandly, "I just checked your rifle and I find it has been fired recently. I'm arresting you for the murder of Davey Lamond. Get onto your horse and ride ahead of me. Drop your gun slow and easy, and remember that the first jump your horse makes gets you a slug in the back."

There couldn't be any doubt now about his intentions. He aimed to frame me for the killing and I figured he could make it stick. He did, too.

We rode into Elk City, with me leading the way and Ash just a few feet behind me. I think he wanted me to make a break, but I didn't oblige him. He locked me up, sent somebody after the body, and then he and another deputy, Briscoe, went through my pockets and my bed roll. By that time, of course, they knew who I was.

I was sure now they'd got the word about me. I also have a hunch that they had word to see that I didn't leave the jail alive. They never said anything about Martin and obviously did not intend to try me for his killing, but they had me for the boy's murder. Naturally nobody much believed me after they heard what Ash had to say.

Like I said before, I don't know what really happened. I'm guessing that John Ash killed the boy, maybe by mistake thinking he was getting the boy's pa. It seems from what Ed has picked up around town that there had been a feud between old man Lamond who had brought some sheep into the county about a year ago and several cowmen who had threatened him.

They have made the point stick that I'm a killer. They've looked up my back trail clear to my stepfather in the Willamette Valley of Oregon. They claim I killed him. They found out about the horse thief in Miles City and the rest on down to Pete Martin. By "they" I mean Ash and Sheriff Swanson and the judge and the prosecuting attorney. Once they had established the fact that I had killed several men, they had no trouble making the jury believe I had been hired by some mysterious, unnamed cowman, who has remained unnamed, to shoot the Lamonds.

I believe it was John Ash who had been hired by the mysterious cowman. I believe Ash killed the boy and hid in the tall sage brush just before I came over the ridge. He must have seen me coming and from the direction I was going, guessed I'd come close enough for him to be able to blame me for the murder.

When I stopped to help the boy, he knew he'd never have a better chance to grab a scapegoat. I haven't told anyone my suspicions except Ed, and he agreed there was no use to tell them because no one would believe me any more than they have believed me when I told the jury what happened. So I've been railroaded, and I'll die for a killing I didn't do.

I've had a feeling all along that no one in Elk City really wanted to know the truth about the boy's murder, that it would kick up a lot of dust for some local men, and nobody wanted that dust raised. All of them are happy they have someone to hang.

The fact that David's father sold out and left the country after the funeral is another indication of what was going on. I don't know whether he believed I did the shooting, but he certainly believed the local cowmen were going to get him if he didn't leave.

As soon as the news of my arrest got into the newspa-

pers and Ed heard about it, he quit his job and came here.
He brought some money from Al Swan for my defense,
but I made Ed send it back. After the way I left Al, I
didn't want a nickel from him. I used my own money, but
I didn't get my money's worth. I had a poor lawyer.
Maybe he was threatened and told to do a bad job. This is
something else about the whole business I don't know,
either. All I do know is that he didn't work very hard at
getting me cleared.

I know something else. The community tried me and
convicted me before the trial started, and now the people
here are determined to execute me so that David Lamond's murder will be officially closed. They don't want it
opened up again, either. It is less uncomfortable to hang
an innocent man than it is to dig out the truth.

I hope these people have one hell of a time from now
on because they deserve it. They know I'm innocent and
they won't forget it. I am going to fool them in one way.
They'll never hang me.

21

PAT BRADY was so absorbed in Rick Patterson's journal that he lost track of time. He finished hours later but remained at his desk, staring at the stack of papers. Patterson had reason to be bitter about the world in which he lived, Brady thought.

The journal threw a great deal of light on the Smith County war. Even granting that some of it had been written with prejudice, the fact remained that here was a piece of grass roots history which probably would never see the light of day unless Brady published it himself. The idea intrigued him. He filled and lighted his pipe, and leaned back in his chair to think about it.

The crack of a rifle from the direction of the scaffold jerked him violently out of his reverie. For a few seconds he sat there, half-paralyzed by a ridiculous thought: *Ed Vernal was trying to free Rick Patterson single-handed.*

He whirled away from his desk, clapped his derby on his head, and rushed out of his office into the hot August sunlight. The people gathered around the scaffold were standing frozen, all staring at the hotel. Brady ran to them, bulled his way through the crowd, and then stood motionless, his breath going out of him with a gasping sound.

Rick Patterson lay sprawled under the noose, his arms flung out, unseeing eyes staring at the sky. He had been shot through the head.

Brady wheeled to the man nearest him and shook him by the arm. He demanded, "What happened?"

"Nobody knows," the man said. "Somebody shot Patterson. We think the bullet came from the hotel. Swanson and his deputies are over there now looking for the killer."

"They were just getting ready to put the noose around his neck when the shot came," another man said. "It was from the roof of the hotel."

"I don't think so," the first man said. "I think it was from a window of the second story."

"Anybody see the flash?" Brady asked. "Or the smoke?"

"No," the third man said, "but I think it was from a window on the first floor next to the lobby."

"No such thing," the second man said belligerently. "I told you I seen the flash. It was from the roof."

Brady knew the man, a small rancher from the lower end of the county who was never noted for his veracity, so Brady didn't believe him on general principles.

"I just can't see no sense in it," one of the men said, ignoring the fellow who claimed to have seen the flash. "In another three minutes he'd have been dead anyhow."

"Must have been old man Lamond," a man said. "I'll bet he sneaked into town without nobody seeing him. He probably wanted to do the job and figured it was his right to beat the state to it."

Turning, Brady walked slowly back to his office. No, it didn't make sense. Like the man said, Patterson would have been dead in another five minutes or less. Then Brady stopped flat-footed in the middle of the dust strip and swung around to stare at the hotel.

Ed Vernal, he remembered, had a corner room on the second floor of the hotel. From there he would have a perfect view of the scaffold. Patterson had written that he was a crack shot with a rifle, and had added something about his shooting the wings off a fly and not touching the fly. This, then, had been Patterson's way of making sure he didn't hang. He had written in his journal that he wasn't afraid of being shot, but he was terrified of hanging.

Brady went on to his office, walking slowly. He thought

this was the biggest test of a man's friendship he had ever heard. Vernal would certainly be caught and tried for the murder of Rick Patterson and they'd wind up hanging him. That was a hell of a way for a good man to end up, Brady thought as he walked into the gloom of his office.

He started to hang up his derby, then he stopped again as sharply as he had when he had seen Patterson's body, his breath again going out of him in a long, sighing sound. Ed Vernal sat in a chair beside the desk, his hat cocked on the back of his head, a cigarette dangling from one corner of his mouth.

Vernal said carelessly, "Howdy, Mr. Brady. I'm glad to see you. I need you, you know."

"Swanson's going to be looking for you," Brady said. "You'd better get on your horse and make dust."

Vernal shook his head. "No. That would be an admission of guilt. That's not the way to beat this game, Mr. Brady. That's why I need you. I'd been sitting here talking to you when you heard the shot. I didn't want to be out there watching my friend hung any more than you did."

"Now you just wait a . . . ," Brady began.

"It's either that or you'll see them hang me," Vernal said. "You don't want that, do you?"

Brady hung his hat up and walked to his desk and sat down. Suddenly he felt tired and very old. He guessed Patterson must have felt like that for a good part of the last ten years. Fighting the organization was enough to make any man feel old, and that was exactly what Brady had to do now. Vernal was right. Brady didn't want to see him hang. Patterson's trial and conviction had been enough.

"How'd you get here?" Brady asked.

"Simple," Vernal answered. "It's all a matter of taking advantage of surprise. They were so intent on stringing Rick up that they couldn't believe what happened. I went down the back stairs and hid the rifle in a broom closet by the back door and ran down the alley. I circled the block and crossed the street. Everybody was still standing there, frozen-like, all of them staring at the hotel. I came down the alley to the back of your office and walked in."

"Now just how in the everlasting hell do you know that nobody saw you cross the street?" Brady demanded.

"I don't know," Vernal admitted, "but if anybody had and if he'd recognized me, he'd have started hollering. I was just somebody in the crowd crossing the street if I was seen."

Brady shook his head. "It's not good enough, Vernal. You can ride out of town and be gone, but I can't. My business is here. If anybody did see you cross the street and I tell Swanson you were sitting right here, they'll crucify me."

"You're absolutely right," Vernal agreed, "but tell me one thing. When you were out there while ago, did you find out what actually happened?"

Brady scratched his head. "Yes and no. The trouble was no one agreed."

"That's how we're going to make this work," Vernal said. "You and me will agree that I've been here all the time. Swanson will believe you."

"I don't know if he will or not," Brady said. "He hates me."

"But you're an influential citizen," Vernal said. "He can't very well accuse you of lying. You've got no ax to grind." He pointed at Patterson's diary. "You say you're going to stay here in Elk City. What about that?"

"It's damned interesting," Brady said. "A lot of people will enjoy reading it and a lot of other people would pay big money to keep it from being published."

"You think you can get it published?"

"If I can't, I'll publish it myself. I was just thinking about it. Maybe it wouldn't be the best looking printing job in the world, but once people start reading it and talking about it, some publishing firm will bring it out."

"You're entitled to all the money you can make out of it," Vernal said. "I'd just like some credit. I pretty much rewrote it, you know. Rick's original journal was, well, let's say it was pretty lean."

"I understand that," Brady said. "Patterson told me much the same thing."

"Just one question," Vernal said. "What will happen to you after you publish the book?"

Brady picked up his pipe and filled it. "They'll hound me out of the county. That's exactly what they'll do. Maybe I'll start a newspaper in Smith County."

"Looks to me like you won't be staying here very long," Vernal said.

Brady glowered at him. He was a bachelor, so he didn't have any family bonds to hold him in Elk City. He knew he could sell his newspaper. He'd had several offers in the last year. More than that, he'd had his bellyful of Elk City politics and with Ole Swanson in particular. He guessed it was time to move.

"Yeah, I reckon you're right," Brady said. "Most country editors do move around." He opened a drawer and dropped Patterson's journal into it. "If Swanson comes in, I don't want him to see that. He'd take it away from me if he knew what it was."

Vernal nodded. "I was afraid that would happen in the jail. Briscoe got pretty nosey a few times, but he's so stupid he never figured out what Rick was doing." He pulled at an ear, questioning eyes on Brady. "Did you get a pretty good idea of Rick and how he thought and felt from the journal?"

"You bet I did," Brady answered. "I felt damned sorry for him, too."

"Well, he brought some of his trouble on himself like we all do," Vernal said. "If he'd taken Lisa a long ways from Wyoming, say to California, the chances are they would never have caught up with him. It would have helped to change his name, but he was a very stubborn man. He said he had committed no crime and he was proud of his name and he wasn't going to change it for anybody."

"I got the feeling that after Lisa's death, he didn't care much about anything," Brady said.

"That's right," Vernal agreed. "I don't know exactly how to explain this because my life is important to me, but Rick's wasn't. I think he had reached the place where he did not want to live, but there had been a time when he lived in New Mexico with Lisa when he was a happy man and the world was a good place to be."

A man said from the doorway. "Well, by God, so this is where you are."

John Ash stood in the doorway, a gun in his hand. He backed up and yelled, "I found him, Ole."

The sheriff came in a moment later. "Well now," he said, "you had us jumping, Vernal. We didn't know where to look for you. I'm arresting you for the murder of Richard Patterson."

"I don't think so, Sheriff," Vernal said. "I wouldn't murder my best friend. I didn't murder anybody. Besides, how could you call it murder when you were going to kill him two or three minutes later?"

"Come on," Swanson said. "Get up out of that chair or we'll drag you out. Drop your gun belt. I don't want no trouble with you."

"You'd better go easy, Ole," Brady said. "It's like Vernal said. He didn't shoot Patterson."

Swanson swung around to face Brady. "I'm telling you, Brady. If you keep kicking dust in my face, I'm going to personally beat the hell out of you. From the day John brought Patterson in, you have been trying to . . ."

Brady held up his hand. "You keep pushing me, Ole, and I'll have some things to say about you and Ash. You jail Vernal and you'll have a case of false arrest on your back, and I'll see to it that he has a better lawyer than Patterson did. We're in the twentieth century now, though you act like you're still living in the nineteenth."

"And just how do you know Vernal didn't shoot Patterson?" Swanson demanded.

"Because he was sitting right there in that chair when I heard the shots," Brady answered.

"You're a damned liar," Swanson bellowed. "If you think you can jam that lie down my throat . . ."

Brady was out of his seat, his jaw jutting forward. "Don't call me a liar, you lunk-headed Swede. Maybe it's time this country had a showdown. If you want it, I promise you some things will come out that you'd rather keep quiet. If you've got any sense, you'll drop this whole business and say the killer escaped."

Ash gripped Swanson's arm. "I hate to agree with the inkslinger, Ole, but he's right. We can't prove Vernal wasn't here when the shot was fired. What difference does it make either way? Patterson was gonna die and that's what he done."

Swanson looked at Ash, then slowly brought his gaze back to Brady. He said reluctantly, "We'll drop it, but I tell you, Brady. I'm going to bust you good before we're done. From now on I'll be looking for a chance."

Swanson and Ash stomped out. Vernal said as if he didn't quite believe it had happened, "We did it. It was Ash who turned the trick. Now why do you suppose he did it?"

"Patterson was right," Brady said. "Ash killed the Lamond boy. He's anxious to let sleeping dogs lie. There's too much that could be brought out to suit him. Like being with the invaders. Chances are we could prove that. Besides, he's feeling too guilty to be comfortable."

Vernal nodded. "Makes sense. Well, I'll be sloping along. I'm heading back to Sundance. Al Swan will want to hear what happened. I'm sorry Rick felt the way he did about Al. Fighting just isn't his way and Rick should have known that. I tried to tell him, but he wouldn't believe it."

"I wondered about that," Brady said as he shook hands with Vernal. "I'll let you know how I make out with the journal. Sundance will be your address for a while?"

"I'll be there for a while," Vernal agreed and, turning, walked out of the office.

Brady sat down at his desk and drew envelopes and writing paper from a pigeonhole. He reckoned the sooner he sold the Elk City Weekly Gazette and got out of the county the better.